*To Bonnie,
Thank you for
book ⊆.
E.*

Wouter F. Nunnink

Ba El Shebub's Gift Awakens

BOOK I –
THE SOUND OF THE GONG

Written by
Wouter F. Nunnink

PublishAmerica
Baltimore

First printing

ISBN: 1-4137-9577-3
PUBLISHED BY PUBLISHAMERICA, LLLP
www.publishamerica.com
Baltimore

Printed in the United States of America

Foreword

The story you are about to read was initially inspired by a distant memory of the tale of Nils Holgersson, written by the Swedish Noble Prize winner Selma Lagerlof. I read it when I was just a youngster myself, but it surfaced in my memory many years later when I retold the story of the adventures of the young boy and the goose to a young friend, Eddie Jn., who happened to be 11 at the time. It became apparent to me that a magical idea like that could be incorporated into a magnificent all-encompassing tale that dealt with the magically-compounded adventures of two youngsters of our time. Thus was conceived a story of a magic that was to affect all mankind, complete with its history, and the events leading to the completion of its designated task.

The adventurous flight of the young man on the back of the goose evolved into a far greater tale. It is a tale about how a subtle yet powerful magic, gifted by an ancient visionary nearly 5000 years ago, awakens; a tale that eventually takes us all around the world. It has grown from a child's fairy tale into a story filled with intrigue and action suitable to a slightly more mature readership. The events and the action in this, and the following stories, are subtly controlled by a magic that, while working through two youngsters as its conduits, is fully intent on its goal to save mankind from its own inequities. Thus, in this story we have blended in all the components of fantasy into the reality of our modern day.

It seemed appropriate to start the telling of this story with this, the 1st book in a series of three volumes. It includes the magical adventures of a young boy, age 11, while traveling on the back of a swan, and those of his younger sister.

The history of the magic leading up to the present time, which is the time during which this first volume plays itself out, will entail the writing of several other volumes. For now the short prologue will have to do.

Dedicated to:

My young friend Eddie Aguilar Jn.
My grandson Nickolas Pelrine
And
My niece Sarah Nunnink
My nephew Tyler Kilburn
My niece Rena Kilburn

Have you seen the magic that comes from the bard's telling?
A story reflected in a young child's wide eyes?
With characters magically alive in visions never shared
Through bounteous imagination and an openness to be
inspired.
In adults mature, reality invested mind, a true respite
With story's fancied flight that taps one's mind's eternal
youth.

Prologue

Even before the rise of the Mesopotamian Empires in the valleys of the rivers Tigris and Uphretes, many years before the rise of the city state of Ur, there were shamans who conjured with magic and attempted to find ways to deal with forces that were supernatural. One of them lived around 2756 B.C. He was Ba El Shebub, a lonely mystic who was also a powerful conjurer. Ba had recurring visions of a future that depicted what might possibly be the end of human life on earth. In one of these visions he saw that the human race had lost control over its own destiny as well as that of other living beings, because there were a few powerful and misguided beings that had the power to dictate who or what would live or die. They also revealed to him that mankind had lost its appreciation for life and living things. Some of those visions showed him things that terrified him because they looked so alien and had unimaginable destructive powers.

Ba El Shebub was disturbed by these powerful visions of a future that predicted the downfall of humanity. His mind was so occupied with them that he decided to take time and get away from the demands placed on him by his people. He spent several months alone at the nearest mountaintop. When he came back, he was blind and had lost the ability to speak. He was so emaciated that his skin hung on his bones in loose folds. Those who took care of him then discovered that his power had increased manifold. He had gained the ability to make his thoughts be known without speech, by making words appear inside people's heads. With the wave of a finger, symbols would appear on the dried, stretched skins they brought to him at his request. Through these symbols and his unspoken words, he informed his young apprentices that he had decided to call for an enclave of the most powerful shamans, conjurers, and sorcerers from as far away as his message could reach. Thus, he sent his pupils off in all the different directions to contact other wise men and shamans with the message to gather on that same mountaintop. He would meet with them there.

After nearly a year of intermittent waiting, they came from near and far. Some came from as far away as India, Mongolia, Africa, Europe, and one from an unknown continent beyond Asia. Many had shared similar visions and had been so disturbed by them that they had started traveling to share their unquiet with others like them. So it was that they came together in the year 2688 B.C. They chose the wisest and most powerful amongst them to form a council whose commission it was to create a powerful and lasting magic. A magic so refined that it would be able to adjust itself to changing times. In that way, when the time came when it was needed, it would be in position to influence changes that might save mankind.

After many months, their combined efforts created a magic that was capable of performing lasting magical feats equaling in variety and subtlety the colors of the rainbow. Guarding spells woven into the silk scrolls upon which it was written would prevent anyone, including the council's own members, from using the magic for their own purposes. In addition, the full power of the magic would allow itself to be invoked only if conditions indicated that humanity was on a course headed toward the cataclysms seen in the visions and a suitable candidate or candidates had been found who could carry out its mission. Until then, it would work itself into the fabric of life, choosing those few who would be allowed limited access to its magic and at the same time creating a separate realm into which those chosen might hide and escape notice.

It was agreed that one spirit alone would accompany the magic over its time-enduring voyage and utter the releasing phrases, or destroy it if that was needed. So it was that Ba El Shebub sacrificed the peace of his soul, committing his spirit to be the magic's guardian.

...As the passing centuries turned into millenniums, Ba's spirit slumbered peacefully while residing inside the bole of an ancient tree located on a rise in a valley just north of an inland ocean we now refer to as the Black Sea. Every once in a while the spirit stirred, awakening just enough to taste the strands of the magic as it traversed the continents, just enough to know that the time had not yet come...

In the thousands of years that came and went, there were a few chosen ones who were given limited access to Ba's magic. It provided for those chosen individuals access to a magic realm safe from worldly intrusions. Inside this realm, individuals would exist in such a reduced state that they would be invisible to other human beings not affected by the magic. In addition, be it a curse or a blessing, aging was slowed down dramatically, so much so that some lived for nearly a thousand years. Unfortunately, most of the individuals who existed within the realm did not have the ability to escape from it and return to the world as we know it. In addition, they were not protected from themselves or from each other. This resulted in many taking on the form of monsters, deformed by the corruption of their own minds.

Only those chosen few who possessed the ability to wield the magic could travel back and forth between the realm and the world as we know it. Those individuals wielded great power within the realm and were usually very influential beings in the world of man as well.

In 1259 A.D. a young merchant named David DeBourbon found the magic tome among hundreds of other tomes in the library of the abbey at Palermo, Sicily. At the time he stumbled onto it, he was helping his good friend Archduke Guiseppi Mephistopheles who was searching for a cure against a deadly outbreak of smallpox.

For more than seven centuries, David and his erstwhile friend maintained control of the magic tome and through it over the realm of magic.

David, who was now called David of Rochelle outside of the magic realm and referred to as the Black Mage within it, soon got bored with life inside the realm. Having acquired mastery of a number of spells, David slipped back and forth between the real world and the realm of magic, in the process acquiring incredible wealth.

Mephistopheles, who had acquired the title of Cardinal while still in the world of man, had brought his Prussian Guardsmen with him when he was forced to take refuge into the magic realm. Over the centuries Cardinal Mephistopheles, his religious zeal eroded and his sense of right and wrong warped, found pleasure in playing cruel games with the denizens of the realm. Because he had very limited control over the magic, he rarely ventured out of the realm of magic.

Four and a half centuries later, in the middle of a Dutch winter in the year 1699, David of Rochelle escaped the tumultuous times in France. He had decided to settle for the peaceful life in Holland. Thus, he arrived at the small but cozy miller's house located next to a large windmill used for grinding flour. Enamored with the miller's wife, David decided to stay at the miller's residence. It did not take very long before the miller, Burgher Jan, mysteriously disappeared. Several months afterward, his 13-year-old daughter Jenn disappeared as well.

A year after marrying the miller's widow, David decided to return to the magic realm, leaving behind the young widow and her newborn son. All that is known of her after that is that she sold the mill and left town.

Many other young couples tried their luck at running a milling business out of the same windmill. When most of them suffered mysterious accidents, the large windmill in its picturesque setting was tagged with the label of being haunted. It stood there suffering silently, while time stripped it of its usefulness.

More than four and a half millenniums have passed since the magic's creation. All the while the spirit of Ba El Shebub maintained its semi-dormant vigil…

…A cold mist swirled through the leaves of the gnarled tree at the top of the rise. From the top of the rise, with the sun just topping the surrounding hills, the valley looked misty and peaceful. Feathery clumps of mist slowly drifted upward, following the valley's gentle slope toward distant hills and mountains.

Ba El Shebub had selected this peaceful site as the most effective, least disrupted location from where his dormant essence could maintain contact with the magic—the very same magic now tugging at his spirit's consciousness.

Contrary to the peacefulness of the pastoral scene, a determined feeling of unrest was tearing away at the magic curtain that had protected his spirit from unwanted intrusions. Torn from its magic slumber within the bole of the old tree, Ba El Shebub's essence was awakened by an urgency not felt for close to 5000 years.

Resentful at the disruption, Ba El Shebub touched the strands of magic to ascertain the need for the intrusion. "Cursed be man's folly that hath thus torn my spirit from its rightful rest," he grumbled. Then, as the impact of the years became clear to Ba's soul, he whispered, "The winds of change have left their mark. Time has been long in passing."

Aided by the magic, Ba's informed spirit became aware of how rapidly mankind had drifted toward his prophetic, cataclysmic visions. Sighing, the spirit exclaimed, "Ah, how great the outward appearance of change. Yet, how numerous what has remained unchanged in man. This time, however, I sense a strain in the ebb and flow of power, as well as in man's respect of the truth of his being."

After a few moments, needed to digest the information acquired by it, the spirit concluded, "Powerful men and women hold rule; some are as ruthless as those of times past. However, their impact on the river of life is far greater. Especially disconcerting is the gathering darkness from the area near where once I called home…an evil intent, spreading fatalistic dogma with the purpose of gaining power in the confusion caused by mindless killing. Fortunately, I sense that all is far from lost, for the forces of reason and compassion are still strong. However, I fear the time has come to release the magic from its binds. If all goes well, there will be a powerful conduit for the magic to do its work. It will require a spirit strong and pure, and a mind agile and receptive. Pray there is at least one."

Thus it was that the spirit of Ba El Shebub uttered the phrases that released constraints from a magic that, when properly invoked by its intended wielder, would be more powerful than any ever unleashed, yet be so subtle no ordinary man would be able to discern its workings; its sole purpose, to help mankind to protect it from itself.

Having completed its task, the spirit of Ba El Shebub resumed its slumber in the knoll of the ancient tree.

In the valley below, the meandering water of the river that drew its life from the foothills of the Caucasus Mountains continued its journey toward the blue waters of the Black Sea.

CHAPTER 1
MURDER BY MAGIC

A ray of sunlight penetrated the darkness inside the old broken down windmill; its light revealed part of a broken beam leaning across the remains of the bulky vertical central axis of what used to be the grinding stone. There was not much left of the upper of the two grinding stones.

Nothing seemed to stir, or break the oppressive silence that reigned within. Yet, things were not what they appeared. Visible only to others in the magic realm, two figures were in a heated discussion among the detritus of broken stone within the bright light of the dazzling sunray.

Burgher Jan used to be the miller who operated this windmill in 1496 before he was tricked into the magic realm by the Black Mage David; dressed in rags and looking much older with a balding head and a stooped frame, he looked tired and defeated.

The other, a strikingly beautiful and athletic blond pixie, was his daughter Jenn. At the time of her father's disappearance Jenn had been only thirteen and the target of David's amorous advances. Unsuccessful in his efforts to secure her love, David had sent her into the magic realm as well hoping that by doing so he would increase his control over her.

It did not work out that way. Becoming more determined with time, Jenn had committed herself to returning her and her father to the world of humans. For this they needed someone who would have the ability to wield the magic. Since the Black Mage David and his partner Cardinal Mephistopheles were not likely to oblige, they needed to find some one who might not only be coaxed into reading the spells, but might also be able to wield its magic. They knew the magic scroll still resided within the confines of the old mill. However, until fairly recently they had been unsuccessful in finding a suitable candidate; that is until Jenn located Aaron Rocher.

Shaking her finger at her father, Jenn addressed him agitatedly, "Father, we can't just openly apply pressure to this man to do our bidding. Aaron Rocher will be the one. I'm sure of it. I believe that he is in some way related to the last family to successfully run this mill."

She turned from him and took a few paces, then rounded on him again. "It's true I've perfected the summons, and I am sure that only those sensitive to the magic, like Aaron Rocher, will respond to it. There's still the possibility that others will have sensed it, too—others who don't mean us well, Father."

She pressed on. "If we do not proceed cautiously, they will find a way to stop us just as they have done time and time again. As a matter of fact, I'm not so sure they aren't on to us already."

It was still fairly quiet inside the large warehouse located on the docks in Amsterdam's harbor. The day crew had not arrived for work as yet. A weak grey light filtered in through the high windows. All appeared peaceful, except that invisible to the human eye two minute individuals were carrying on a rather one-sided discussion. It was dominated by the larger and bulkier of the two. With his hooded crimson cape covering what appeared to be a floor length and gown-like purple cope, Cardinal Mephistopheles paced back and forth on the broad windowsill. His cape billowing out behind him, he wheeled to turn back on the other. "Why are you so hesitant to put a firm stop to their interference?" For a moment the burning yellow eyes flared visibly under the large hood that covered his head while they focused on the other seated comfortably in the nook of the window.

Wrapped in a black cloak, the second figure appeared to be lost in thought while staring out into the grey morning mist. He was clean shaven; the powerful nose and bushy eyebrows created deep pools of shadows centered by sparkling, coal black eyes. He appeared to be paying little heed to the agitated figure pacing in front of him.

Clearly frustrated, close to anger, the crimson apparition growled, "David, don't you see what they are trying to do? The girl and her father are determined to undermine our control of the realm. I can't allow them that privilege! They need to be taught their place!"

Waking up from his reverie, the black-cloaked figure raised his dark, time-worn face; coal black sparkling eyes took in the apparition in crimson and purple towering over him. When he spoke, it was in a soft, level voice completely in control. "Your Eminence, I really do not see a threat here. I am firmly in control of the magic and I don't see how that is going to change. Our spies could be wrong about Aaron Rocher's involvement. We could be overreacting by acting now. Maybe we would be better off to wait and see."

Averting David's gaze, the cardinal started to turn away, then changed his mind and whirled back to face the Black Mage. As he did, the swirl of the cape and the movement of the long cope underneath seemed to reveal the presence of a third appendage. It appeared to twitch like a tail, revealing the agitation of its owner. "David, unlike you I cannot put the fear I feel aside. I feel like Saul faced with his vision. Except in mine, I see a wrathful God waiting for me to be forced out of this realm where I have been like a God, waiting to blast my soul into eternal hell."

Pacing back and forth restlessly he continued, "David, I'm scared of what will happen to us if you lose control of the magic, as frightened as I was when you rescued me and my loyal guardsmen from sure death at the hands of that Judas, King Louis XIV, more than 700 years ago. If it hadn't been for your magic rendering us invisible, and so minute that we could walk right through the walls of our prison, we would have died the same death as that poor martyr, Pope Bonafice." Momentarily lost in reflection, he crossed himself. With his hands still clutching the ornate cross at his chest, he continued, "It is God's will that we are who we are. I will not fail to make sure that things stay this way."

In spite of the weather the Dutch city of Amsterdam was bustling, its citizens so used to rainy weather that the misting rain hardly slowed them down. Out near the port, large ships were passing through the locks as fast as they could manage.

One of thousands working the busy docks of the harbor, Aaron Rocher was the operator of one of the huge off-loading cranes. He had been at this job, loading and unloading huge loads for many years. For him, on the job incidents had been few and when they did occur they were fairly insignificant.

He liked his high perch inside the glass cab far removed from the hustle and bustle of the docks. Next to the controls he handled with the deft skill of many years of experience, he had placed a picture of his family: his lovely wife Gemma and his two young children, Aarvid and Mona. When things were not that busy, looking at them inspired daydreams of the cozy house next to the canal where he would hold them in his arms or playfully jostle them. He would remember their happy faces smiling back at him, or dream of the upcoming weekend's activities they had planned out. Most recently, he seemed to have been especially drawn to bring his wife and the kids swimming, and picnicking in the grass next to the pond that partially surrounded the old windmill.

Today, however, there was a boat to unload. It was overcast and wet. Aaron was not too fond of the misty rain that was falling; the droplets were so tiny they would settle on his window until the wipers cleared a large swath, only to have the steady mist cover them almost immediately. It made it more challenging to control the heavy loads being lifted by the tall crane. With warehouses filled with dockworkers on one side and large ships, their own shorter cranes working on the other, it was essential that the huge, towering cranes and their oversize loads were properly controlled as they passed over and onto the crowded docks.

Perched on the edge of his seat, his attention was fully focused on the end of the cable with its large orange hook. Swinging it around, he kept the cable short to keep it under control until it was almost directly above its target. Responding to the hand signals of the ship's deck officer, he lowered it slowly into the hold of the lumber transport.

After the load was secured, Aaron raised it high into the air, shortening the cable and giving him better control, while insuring that the load would clear all obstacles.

Standing on the broad sill of one of the upper windows of an adjacent warehouse, two men, invisible to anyone but those in the magic realm, watched the tall crane operated by Aaron as it lifted its load high into the air.

"Are you certain you want to go through with this, Your Excellency?" The question was voiced with great urgency by the black cloaked figure. David knew they had reached the moment of no return. He eyed his bulky, crimson cloaked companion who was intently watching the working crane.

"David, we have got to slam the door on them hard. By removing the object of their hope we remind them that we are the magic realm, and will continue to be!" Raising his hands as if delivering a sermon, his focus still on the moving crane, he continued, "The scourge must be wiped out cleanly. There is nothing more sublime than purging by fire. So it shall be!" With raised hands, that were now aimed palms out toward the tall specter of crane #3, Mephistopheles cried out an unintelligible chant.

As his hands deftly manipulated the levers that shifted the gears to turn the cab and with it the towering boom with its load, Aaron was distracted by a crackling and hissing sound. It took only a moment for him to realize that there was a fire in the control panel attached to the rear of the cab.

Along with the crackle of the electrical fire and the acrid smoke entering into the cab, another new sound entered his awareness. The whine of the cable running through its tackle at increasing speeds forced his attention back to the load. To Aaron's horror the load was descending out of control. Instinctively engaging the emergency brake with both hands to stop the descending load, Aaron pulled with a desperation born from the realization that something had gone very wrong.

Desperately clinging to the brake, his lungs burning and his eyes watering from the sharp acrid smoke, Aaron observed through the smoke and the mist covered window that while the load had nearly stopped its rapid descend, it was now like a large wrecking ball rapidly closing in on his glass-enclosed cab. Determined to save the lives of others down on the ground, he continued to cling to the emergency brake.

Outside on the docks someone shouted, "The #3 crane is on fire!" Almost immediately it was followed by another voice, "Watch out! Its load is out of control!"

For a few moments chaos reigned on the busy dock. People scrambled away from the more dangerous places. Next silence, followed by murmurs, and finally shouts of renewed alarm as some in the crowd pointed out the struggling figure inside the smoke- filled cab. They all watched the pendulum swing of the large load headed right for the glass cab. For a moment it seemed that everything was happening in slow motion. The crash and explosion of flames as the pine beams impacted the cab brought a renewed hush from the watching crowd before they exploded in a frenzy of activity. The drama temporarily forgotten, they busied themselves fighting the infernal flames before it could spread and engage the rest of the dock.

Back on the windowsill of the storehouse, David watched as the load of pine timbers was about to strike the cab of crane #3. At the very moment of impact, he turned away from his companion and uttered a few words of magic of his own. For a moment, it appeared that time itself had stopped. Then, softly uttering another quick phrase, he thrust his hand in the direction of the crane.

Mephistopheles, believing it to be an expression of

celebration, clasped the hand in both of his own and raised them skyward.

The expression on his face reflecting ecstasy, he shouted, "It is done! David, it is done! We have erased their little dream in a cleansing of fire!"

His hysterical laugh caused a momentary look of concern on David's face.

The abrupt, "Let us get ourselves back to our havens," signaled the end of his mirth. Turning in a flurry of scarlet and purple, Mephistopheles headed back into the dark interior of the warehouse.

David did not follow. "Go ahead, Your Excellence. I'll catch up soon. There are a few loose ends I have to attend to."

Watching the bulky crimson apparition nod as he moved off, David turned and headed for the opening in the window.

All that remained of crane #3 was the intact base upon which rested the charred, twisted remains of the cab and boom structures.

There was nothing anyone could have done to save Aaron Rocher. Before anyone had a chance to sound the alarm, the huge load of lumber had torn through the flaming cab. The inferno that ensued, so hot, no one could come near enough to soak it down. All efforts had to be directed at keeping the fire from spreading. When finally the fire-tugboats engaged the flames from the water, there was nothing left to save but some charred pieces of lumber.

Officially they called it an accident. However, a few who had witnessed the inferno expressed their suspicion that a small bomb or incendiary device might have been the cause of the fire. Not one of the hundreds of dock workers who had come to pay their respects mentioned their suspicion to the grieving widow. Heartbroken, standing between her young son and daughter, they knew it was difficult enough for her to have to deal with her husband's death.

Invisible to the crowd, two tiny figures looking down from the vantage of an air duct shared her grief. Burger Jan, looking even older and more bend, listened distractedly to his youthful looking daughter. "I am sorry that things worked out so badly, Father," she said while tears coursed down her cheeks.

"Me, too, child." A deep sigh accompanied the old man's somber response. "If we could have kept our effort a secret just a little longer, we might now be back in the real world." He nodded at the gathering in the large room.

"If only I could have been there to warn him," she sobbed. "Maybe..."

She was cut off by the gesture of the old man as he raised both hands in a warding move, "Jenn, it was not our doing. We are not to blame. The guilt lies with the evil ones. They don't want to risk any threat to their power. Aaron Rocher could have worked the spells only after he had a chance to study the book. We never got as far as getting him to the book!"

Straightening himself and taking a deep breath, he continued pleadingly. "Jenn, we only got as far as making him interested in going near that cursed old mill, to fish and swim with the kids. Look what it got us. They killed him!"

CHAPTER 2
THE WINDMILL

The Rocher family lived in a small cottage abutting the earthen dam that ran along the length of a well-used canal. It was early Saturday morning, but already sounds from the traffic on the water, hidden by the raised dike, filtered down into the kitchen where Gemma Rocher was frying small sugar-dusted dough cakes for a freckled nine-year-old, with an unruly tousle of auburn hair cropped just below her ears. Hearing the sound of the voices on the canal, Mona perked up from her silent breakfast. "Mom, can I go to the canal to see the boats?"

"Not before finishing your chores, dear, and especially not by yourself," Gemma responded while lovingly running her fingers through the nape of her daughter's lush and soft hair.

Gemma loved the weekends. It gave her a chance to spend some time with her children. Having them around made the house seem less empty. Even though it had been six years since the tragic death of Aaron Rocker, her husband, his loss still filled her with a painful emptiness.

In her two children, she recognized many of his features and mannerisms. Especially in Aarvid who, approaching his twelfth birthday, reminded her more and more of his father even though everyone else seemed to recognize his mother's good looks in him.

As the late summer sun send golden beams of light through the dormer into Aarvid's bedroom, he stretched lazily in his bed and watched bright specks of dust floating through the bright rays. At eleven he was the oldest and had been given his own bedroom in the converted attic. Since it was Saturday, he could stay in bed as long as he wanted. But, a look through the window made him excited about the promise of another warm summer-like day. Standing in front of the window, stretching the stiffness out of his lean body in the warm sunlight, he could clearly see the dark spokes of the old windmill as they stretched skyward in the distance beyond the green of nearby trees. The sight evoked mixed emotions, reminding him of the pleasure of swimming in the pond adjoining it, as well as apprehension evoked by the stories of its curse.

Responding to the banging of the outside door below his room, Aarvid opened his window. The cool morning breeze ruffled his unruly, light brown hair as he leaned forward to look out. Below in the yard, Mona was already busy with her chores.

At the sound of the window opening, she looked up at her brother hanging out of the window, and shouted, "Hey, lazybones, what are you doing hanging out of the window stark naked?"

Before Aarvid could sputter back a retort, she resumed, "Aren't you going to get down here to help me? I want to get these chores done so I can do some fishing before it gets too warm!" Personally, she favored chatting with passing boats men. She knew, however, that fishing, one of her brother's favorite pastimes, would rouse him more quickly.

He leaned his tanned body out through the window and reached his arm out toward her, shouting, "I'll be right down if you wait for me!"

"OK." With that, she continued to drag the trash bag across the yard, to the trash shed behind the house. But before she had taken two steps, half turning and chuckling slightly, she added, "And put on some clothes! You're scaring off all the animals as well as the neighbors!"

It didn't take long for Aarvid to throw on a pair of shorts, gobble down a plate of sugar dusted dough cakes, down a glass of milk, and complete his chores.

His mouth still stuffed with the remains of the poffertjes, white sugar powder clinging to the corners of his mouth, he hugged his mother. "Mom, we're going to be at the bridge fishing for a while. OK?"

"Sure, my big guy," Gemma responded, returning his hug by pressing him to her body. "But please keep an eye on Mona. Sometimes she gets a little too carefree with strangers." Unable to resist the temptation to try and settle his unruly light brown mop, she ran her hands through it. Cut a little shorter than his sister's, it seemed to have a mind of its own sticking up and out in different directions.

He tolerated her caressing ministrations for a moment. Then, while turning and walking away from her, he responded, "I will, Mom; you know I always do."

Watching him walk off, Gemma reflected on the changes she had noticed in him. More than ever he had started looking like a teenager. Already tall for his age, he had begun to develop physically in ways that reminded her of his father who had been 6'3, lean and well muscled.

After a couple of hours of fishing underneath the draw bridge that crossed the canal, Mona, who had lost interest and was carrying on a conversation with a passing boatman, spotted Anke and Wim. They were riding down the bike path toward her. Mona could see that they were wearing their bathing suits and carried towels.

"Hi, Mona," shouted Anke, stretching and looking around, trying to catch a glimpse of Aarvid. "Where is your brother?"

"Yeah, hi, Mona," added Wim. "Where is he? I don't see him."

Aarvid, who had heard the commotion, shouted up to them from the shadows under the bridge, "Hi, guys! I'm down here fishing. I'll be right up!"

In the meantime, in the magic realm and within the collapsed ruins of what once was the Miller's house next to the old windmill, Jenn was having another agitated discussion with her father.

Burgher Jan was looking worried. Unhappy with Jenn's reasoning, he retorted heatedly, "How can it be safer for the two children to be introduced to the magic now, rather than when they are more grown up? I think you are making a big mistake, big enough for all of us to pay for with our lives!"

Equally excited she retorted, "Papa, you remember what they did to their father! Unless they have the use of the magic to protect themselves, his children will suffer the same fate! I don't intend to sit back and wait until these two innocent children suffer fatal accidents!"

Seemingly resigned, more bent over than ever, he shook his

head at her and said, "Jenn, I think you are making a big mistake by risking these two youngsters." Sighing, "I don't want any part of this!"

Still shaking his head he disappeared into the darkness behind one of the many loose bricks scattered around the remains of the house.

"Aarvid, see that big fat swan hiding in the rushes over there?" asked Anke. They were swimming side by side in the middle of the pond. She had been trying all afternoon to get Aarvid to pay closer attention to her. He had seemed distracted somehow and that bothered her more than she wanted to admit.

"Let's sneak over there and scare it right out of the water."

"Nah, I'd rather not," he replied without enthusiasm. "I like that swan. It's like a pet to me. He eats the little snacks I bring for him right out of my hand."

"How do you know it's a He and not a She?" she asked, feigning interest.

"I just know," he replied, sighing as if bored.

Aarvid could not explain why he felt so distracted today. He really liked Anke; the attention she gave him usually made him feel strangely warm inside. He liked that strange, yet confusing feeling. Today, however, was just not the same. It was as if Anke was intruding…on what he really was not sure.

"I think I might just go inside that old windmill and check it out." It was out before he realized what he was saying. The urge to explore the windmill was suddenly extremely strong. It was as if someone was pulling him toward it.

"Aarvid, don't!" The concern in her voice was so genuine it made him turn around to face her. Threading water, Anke looked him in the eyes, and sounding seriously concerned asked, "Don't you remember all the stories that people tell about that place? It's probably haunted."

At a loss to explain to her his sudden urge to explore the windmill, Aarvid started swimming back toward the little wooden landing where Mona and Wim were stretched out lounging, and talking.

While Aarvid and Mona were swimming with their friends outside in the bright summer sun under the looming structure of the old wind-mill, inside, in the dark and dank confines of the old mill, another scene was playing itself out. Within the starkly different dimensions of the magic realm, Jenn found herself trapped and was about to be engaged in a fight for her life.

With her golden hair tied in a ponytail, and her slim figure dressed in homemade jeans and a tattered blouse, she looked a sharp contrast and frail compared to the two creatures she was facing; both of them were armed and wearing pieces of insect chitin for protective armor.

Quickly, she assessed her situation. Her mobility was severely limited by the small space formed by a downward slanting section of wallboard overhead and almost solid walls of chunks of millstone and metal pieces that supported it. The one opening offering escape was guarded by the largest of her attackers holding a sword-like weapon. Her other adversary, a gnome like creature, tried advancing on her through the part of her trap that was the most confining because of its low ceiling.

Outwardly, her lean and athletic figure, holding a weapon in each hand, presented a picture of pure determination. Inwardly, Jenn was feeling anxiety close to despair. How could she have allowed herself to be trapped in this tight a spot? How could they have anticipated where she would be?

Crouching low, firmly clutching a sharp edged rock in her left, she used her right hand to jab a sharp, pointed piece of metal the length of her forearm at the closest one of her attackers. Maintaining her crouch, ready to respond quickly, she thrust the sharp, pointed metal at the grotesque humanoid.

Changed by many years spent inside the magic realm, it had become a reflection of its true character; a killer with a snout-like face, it crawled in the confining space on its knobby yet muscular arms and legs and tried raking her with its long, claw-like nails.

Jenn realized that, advancing as it was through the cramped crawl spaces, it could not really do her much harm. Its real purpose was to flush her out of her corner toward his hulk of a partner, so that they then could attack her from two sides. She wondered where her father could be. Why was he not here to help her? How could she extricate herself from this situation?

In her desperation she could think of only one possible way. Her gift from living in the magic realm, aside from her undiminished good looks and youthful appearance, had been the power of mental telepathy; stronger than most, she had developed a method to make mental contact with a few humans outside the realm. She grasped at that as a way to create a possible distraction. With all the intensity her mind could muster, she reached out to the unsuspecting Aarvid. Whispering the suggestion in his mind, *Aarvid, you need to explore the mill! Do it NOW!*

In spite of his friends' and sister's best efforts to convince him not to, Aarvid was undaunted. He was determined to go inside the old windmill and discover for himself what was inside. Still dripping water and wearing nothing but his swimming shorts, he started for the mill.

A reminder of a different era, the bulky windmill looked beaten down and abandoned. With two of the four still impressive wings towering above him, Aarvid took in the surrounding scene while he approached. The pond and its tall rushes in the foreground on his left, the ruins of the cottage on his right, while behind it all farmland stretched as far as the eye could see. Altogether it provided a serene and pastoral setting.

He remembered that it was said that once it was an important mill, used to grind flour, until the miller and his daughter were murdered. Since then, many had tried unsuccessfully to make a go of it. It had fallen on disrepair and supposedly had been haunted by the ghosts of the murdered.

Aware that someone was following close behind him, Aarvid turned to find Mona only a step behind. The Question was clearly written in the expression on her face as she looked up at him. Apologetically, half turned around to face her, he explained, "I just want to see…uh, explore in there."

They continued together through the uncut grass. Where once there had been a walkway skirting the pond, now wildflowers bloomed and tall grasses grew. Aarvid moved carefully on his bare feet through the waist-high growth. Holding on to Mona's hand, he was careful to stay clear of areas with tall rushes indicating the muddy outlines of the pond which stretched all the way to the windmill, nearly touching it where one of the mill's four wings pointed down.

Something moved on the periphery of his field of vision. A quick glance through the tall rushes on his left revealed the white swan following them on the open water of the pond.

Up close, the windmill was even larger than what it appeared to be from the other side of the pond. Towering over his head, its tattered wings like giant paddles that reached way up into the sky, it was an impressive and bulky structure. Aarvid felt intimidated by its size. For a moment he was unsure about proceeding.

His momentary hesitation was swept away by a greater urge

to continue and explore the interior behind the large weather-beaten door. Slightly ajar, with the white paint mostly peeled from its weathered and split wooden surface, it looked far from inviting.

Aarvid, more awed than frightened, his heart pounding in his chest, again asked himself what he was doing here. Somewhat reassured by his sister's touch, the need to go on once again rose inside of him. Before entering, he looked back to where he had left their friends. Far off on the other side of the pond, he could see them still standing on the wooden ramp. They made no sound; holding on to each other they watched. The silence that surrounded him and his sister was slightly unnerving. Mona, still clutching his hand and not saying a word, once again gave him that questioning look.

Aarvid did not answer. Once again seized by that unexplainable urge to go inside and explore, he turned and reached for the doorknob.

The stillness was suddenly shattered by the flapping of wings and the high pitched fluting of the excited swan. Turning his head at the sound, Aarvid could see the large white bird nearby in the pond. It was making that high, penetrating noise; wings flapping, it raised its extended body from the water with its head stretched out, pointing skyward. Aarvid was slightly taken aback by the scene. Could it be trying to warn him? Was it concern he recognized in its eyes?

Overcoming caution, he pushed hard against the door. It swung open slowly, just enough to let them step inside before it got stuck. He entered cautiously, careful of where he placed his bare feet on the dirty rubble-strewn floor. As he took another step into the dark interior, he realized that he was no longer holding onto Mona. His senses told him she was following close behind.

CHAPTER 3
THE DISCOVERY

In a small cave located in a hillside, south, near the Belgian border, a meeting was taking place between the two current powers of the magic realm. Considering it involved two old friends, the meeting was charged with an unusual tension.

Mephistopheles appeared particularly agitated, dressed in his customary deeply hooded crimson cape which covered a floor-length purple cope, he strutted around on a slightly elevated, dirt filled platform. In the semidarkness of the poorly illuminated space his glowing eyes were clearly visible from under the deep shadow of the hood as they changed from a simmering bright yellow to a fire-like orange. "David, you must be on to them by now. They are not going to give it up until they have jeopardized our control of the realm." Clearly frustrated, close to anger he continued in a growl, "That devil's spawned pair forced us into killing the father some years ago when they were about to reveal the secret of the old mill. Now, my spies tell me, they are in the vicinity of that windmill again."

Striding back and forth in front of his seated audience, his tail-like appendage moving sinuously under the cover of the cope, he grumbled worriedly, "They must have knowledge of the presence of the book of spells. But who?...Could it be they are somehow trying to involve the children?"

David, the Black Mage, was seated in the curve of a small branched offshoot of the major root that outlined the raised dais. A worn, black mantle covered his reclining form. After taking a deep sighing breath, he responded, "Your Eminence, they're definitely an annoyance, and I am at a loss to explain how they keep eluding capture. What is particularly disconcerting, because it is unusual, is the fact that it is almost as if the magic is working against me."

Getting up to face his hulking partner, David raised his hands palms up to emphasize the question. "Your Eminence, what are your intentions about this situation?"

"With your consent, David, I will loosen my entire garrison on them. I have already dispatched some of my best mercenaries to try and trap them. I am not going to hold anything back this time. I'll send both Kirchner and Crawitz this time. If Our Lord wills it, I will try to find a way to get to that worm-eaten old windmill myself." Upon completing the sentence he turned, moving away in a flurry of cape and cope, indicating that for him their meeting had ended.

Watching the hulking figure, trailing the extra appendage, descend the irregular steps, David had one more question. "What are your orders to them this time? Are they to kill, or are they to spare that beautiful, spirited, and impossible girl?"

Slowing, half turning toward his black cloaked companion, the Cardinal growled, "Like a bad sin, she is still in your blood. Is she not? But like a bad sin, it is time to exorcize it! May God have mercy on her and her useless father!"

With that as his final comments, he strode away toward the daylight that filtered in through the narrow cave opening, leaving David pensively staring after him.

Momentarily distracted by her effort to reach out mentally to Aarvid, Jenn was brought back to the immediate danger she faced by a voice speaking in a raw, keening pitch. "I'm going to make you mine, you pretty thing!"

The words were spoken by the smaller rat-like gnome. While it spoke, its snout-like mouth revealed large, filed fangs. As if to emphasize the point, a large red-pink tongue, dripping saliva, licked its pale, thin lips.

Almost immediately the larger creature guarding the exit barked out a garbled threat. The initial response of the smaller creature was to shrink away into the low crawling space it occupied. Then, showing defiance, it raised its ugly snout-like face and yawned, showing off rows of sharp teeth.

Jenn knew she had no chance to meet the challenge facing her in a strictly physical manner. Trapped the way she was in the far corner of a somewhat triangular room, she had little room to maneuver and use her quickness. Wearing no protection other than her tattered homemade clothes and sandals, she could not allow herself to receive any type of direct blow. If she was going to get out of this mess it was going to be through her wits, her ability to use her appearance to distract and divide her attackers, along with what weapons she wielded.

Keeping alert to respond to any attempt to attack her, she took in her situation once more looking for anything that might be of use. Behind the hulking form guarding her only escape, she could see the entrance to her cave-like trap outlined in the faint light. Clearly visible in that light were crisscrossing strands of a net-like spider web that covered most of the entrance. Several grotesque, bulbous-eyed skeletons that were ensnared in it moved slowly with the movements of the net as if still alive. It was not a very uplifting scene. Yet, Jenn who had lived an eternity in this world of nightmares could already see a way to escape.

"Which one of you two big, brave warriors will be the first to get him speared on my sword?" As she spoke she lowered her pointed metal weapon and directed it at the smaller of the two. "It will take a lot more than a couple of misfits like you two to take me!" As she said it, she fainted a thrust at the smaller, crawling form. In response it cowered and slunk away into some low crawl space formed by the slanting ceiling. Suddenly reversing herself, she turned her weapon on the big brutish opponent, who was just then trying to advance on her. Caught in mid stride, desperate to escape the pointed end of her weapon, he stumbled backward. Having gained the extra space, Jenn reared back with her rock hand and with all the power she could muster threw it at the smaller opponent who was just then trying to crawl out of its confining space. The rock struck the gnome-like creature squarely below the eye, opening a large and bloody gash. Shrieking in pain and fury it shrunk back against the lowering ceiling, shaking its bloodied head and spraying red blood in all directions.

At that very moment the silence inside was broken by the sound of flapping wings and the excited high pitched squawk of the swan just outside the mill. A few moments later, it was followed by the loud crunching and groaning noise of the door opening. It opened nearly halfway before stopping with another protesting sound. Light flooded through the half opened door into the semidarkness of the mill. It was partially blocked by two slender forms that shuffled cautiously through the opening.

Jenn was ready to use the distraction. She had been waiting

for this since her urgent summons of Aarvid. So, she was prepared to take advantage of what was sure to capture her assailants' attention.

Her larger opponent, temporarily sidetracked by the apparitions in the doorway, had taken his eyes off Jenn. Instantly, she went on the attack, pouncing on the large muscular brute; her attempt to pierce his chest with her weapon was only partially successful as it glanced of one of his ribs, tearing through flesh. Howling from the pain, anxious to get away from her painful jab, the large mass of chitin covered muscle lunged itself backward, out through the narrow opening and into the tattered web, temporarily ensnaring itself.

With escape from her trap no longer blocked, Jenn darted past the struggling creature and turned, running as quickly as her feet could carry her over the debris littered floor toward the darkest corner in the back of the mill. While negotiating the many obstacles scattered in her path, she again focused on the one part of the magic she could wield; using her mental telepathy once more, while disappearing into a passage hidden under pieces of broken wall sections, she whispered into his mind, *Aarvid, search out the secret door, invisible in the darkness in the back of the mill.*

As she broke off the mental contact, she felt a slight drag on her mind. Instantly, she realized how they had been able to locate her. The mages had used her limited use of magic to track her. With that realization came the knowledge that she had bought herself little time and a heap of trouble. Soon, there would be more like the two she had been dealing with and before long a whole horde of evil creatures would be after her and after Aarvid and his sister as well. Doubt tugged at her conscience and raised questions like: *Am I putting the two young ones in too great a danger by continuing to expose them?*

With the evil ones on to my plan, should I still go ahead and introduce Aarvid to the book of magic?

Crawling and leaping over large and small chunks of debris, she reminded herself what happened to his father. Softly, breathing heavy from the exertion, she mumbled, "No, never again will they hurt anyone in that family, not if I can help it."

After passing through a small crack in the wall separating the large interior of the mill from a small backroom, Jenn entered the dark interior of what long ago used to be the private workroom of the man she knew then as David Rochelle. Denizens of the Magic Realm now referred to him as The Black Mage.

Inside the darkened room, the floor was covered knee deep in a blanket of fluffy dust motes. Obstacles of varying size were scattered everywhere which made progress slow and cumbersome. Struggling to keep as fast a pace as possible, Jenn moved on toward the back of the workroom and the workbench. Placed where it was against the back wall, she could just barely make it out. She was determined to gain the workbench ahead or at least at the same time as Aarvid and Mona.

The urgency of her movements concealed her inward struggle. Jenn knew that she had reached an important crossroad in her life and in that of young Aarvid, and possibly his younger sister Mona as well. How could she be certain that the best protection for Aarvid and Mona against the two most powerful mages to rule the magic realm would be to control at least some of its magic? Was she just thinking selfishly? Maybe she could use her suggestive powers to scare them off before it was too late. Once again, she reminded herself of the fate suffered by their father. Bolstered by that memory, determination once again took hold of her.

"I've got to find a way to make him use the book of spells to enter the magic realm." The words were out of her mouth before she realized it. It was as if someone had spoken them for her. She was taken with the idea and shrugged off the strange way in which it had come to her.

How was she going to accomplish such a feat? After all, she was no mage herself. How was an eleven-year-old boy like Aarvid, or for that matter his nine-year-old sister, going to invoke any sort of spell?

As she struggled to make headway toward the workbench, her mind suddenly cleared. A confidence she did not know she possessed replaced all her doubts. "Take it one step at a time," she heard herself say. "First, get him to open the book of magic."

Newly resolved, her mind reached out for his. *Aarvid, look for the door. It's hidden in darkness. Look into the darkness! Look!*

It took a few moments before Aarvid's eyes could adjust to the semi-darkness inside the windmill. Gradually, he could make out some of the details. A narrow beam of light spilling through a hole in the cap of the old mill clearly illuminated a large broken support beam slanting downward at an angle. Its fall had shattered the millstones; pieces of rubble were strewn all over the floor. Dusty spider webs were hanging almost everywhere. No living thing seemed to have disturbed the interior for a very long time. Stepping gingerly alongside of him, Mona was the first to break the silence. "Wow, it's pretty gross in here!"

Anticipating what she was going to say next, and responding to an increased sense of urgency, Aarvid moved on. Shuffling his feet carefully, wincing as sharp rock fragments stabbed his soles, and brushing aside cobwebs with dried up insect bodies suspended in them, he advanced deeper into the darker reaches of the mill.

As his eyes adjusted to the half-light, he noticed that one corner of the large room remained cloaked in darkness. It was there that he felt drawn to the most. He managed to reach that back area of the mill by climbing over another slanting piece of support beam. Any further progress was blocked by a loose, partially fragmented, slanting section of wall that must have fallen down. The eerie silence was broken only by their shallow breathing and the rolling noise of the debris moved by their shuffling feet while they both checked out their surroundings and contemplated what to do next.

Aarvid felt compelled to investigate what was hidden behind the broken wall section. He was about to pull it aside by reaching through the cobwebs with his right hand, when Mona tugged hard on his left and whispered pleadingly, "Aarvid, don't go in there! I want to go back! I am scared! This place is creepy!"

Her plea temporarily shook him out of his trance-like state. As he turned to face his little sister, she snuggled up to him, firmly clutching his hand to her chest. It struck him how tiny and frail she looked framed by the spacious interior and the dark outline of the huge gear-shaft descending from the high upper reaches. "Stay here, sis," he said reassuringly as he managed to retrieve his hand from her grasp. Sounding more distracted, and staring into the dark interior, he continued, "I've just got to see what's back there now that we've gone this far."

Mona couldn't believe what had come over her gentle, careful brother. "This is so unlike him," she whispered to herself. "Why is he doing this?"

"There's got to be something behind all this," mumbled

Aarvid as he moved around obstacles to get a better hold of what proved to be two broken sections of wall. He finally located a place where he could grab hold of one of the sections; pulling on it firmly, he discovered to his relief that it was light and broke apart easily. After moving the broken pieces out of his way and tossing them aside, Aarvid moved slowly and carefully into the dark and recessed part of the mill.

He suddenly realized that Mona was not right behind him. When he turned, he saw her, outlined by the light of the half opened door inside the gloomy, uninviting atmosphere of the mill, standing all by herself. There was just enough light for Aarvid to see the frown on her face that showed her inner struggle to remain where she was, or to follow.

It did not feel right to have her remain where she stood. Speaking softly, as if reluctant to disturb the oppressive silence, he half whispered, "Sis, why don't you go back outside and wait for me." Expecting her to do as he had suggested, he turned back to face the barely visible back wall of the mill.

As his eyes adjusted to the sparse light, he could just make out the outline of a door. After struggling over many obstacles, he managed to reach it.

Aarvid grabbed a firm hold of the door knob and pulled. To his surprise, after some initial resistance, it opened with a groan revealing another dark and uninviting space.

Not exactly knowing why, he felt really excited about his discovery. Hardly hesitating, he stepped through the doorway letting the darkness envelop him. Once inside, he could see that he was in a small square-shaped room. Faint light filtered through tiny cracks in the exterior wall.

Carefully, he shuffled deeper into the room. His feet encountered small objects, and what felt like books and dried up pieces of paper. Against the back wall, he could barely make out the faint outline of a workbench.

Just as he started toward it, a small noise behind him pulled him up short and made him turn around abruptly. Recognizing Mona, who had followed him into the dark little room, he started to let out a sigh of relief but was caught in mid-breath by a sudden, dry scraping noise. Once again turning quickly, he could see nothing that would account for it between him and the workbench.

As he started again toward the back of the room and the workbench, the scraping noise could be heard again. This time, Aarvid realized that is was coming from the outside. Instead of feeling weak with fear by the creepiness of the place, he felt stimulated; even so, the mix of anxiety and excitement raised the hair on the back of his neck and gave him goose bumps.

By feeling his way carefully around the many objects that were scattered on the floor, he managed to reach the workbench without too much difficulty. Against the back wall, just above the workbench, he could just discern the outline of what must have been a shuttered window. Mona, who now was leaning up against him, reached out to touch some of the larger objects on the work bench before joining him in a careful exploration of the other objects scattered on its surface.

"Boy, what a mess," was her first reaction. "There's nothing but bottles, books, and other junk all over this…this, uh…table." She sounded intrigued and not quite as scared.

"I think it's a workbench," he responded softly. Still half whispering, almost as if talking to himself, "I'd like to see what these things are." Then, more excitedly, "Maybe I can reach that window up there, open it up and let in some light." As he started to place his hands on the counter, he was reminded of the clutter. "First we've got to clear away some of this stuff, so I can climb up on this bench."

Together, they moved aside what felt like empty and half-filled bottles, and heavy, musky smelling books. A few minutes later, Aarvid had one knee on top of the counter and was stretching as far as he could to reach one of the wooden planks that covered the shuttered window. After a couple of unsuccessful tugs it gave way with a groan. Pulling with both hands, Aarvid managed to open enough of a space to let in sufficient light for them to see clearly. A welcome rush of fresh air cleared away the stale, musty smell.

Seated on top of the counter, quite pleased with himself, Aarvid surveyed the little room. It was cluttered with bookshelves containing large numbers of books and artifacts; some had fallen, spilling their contents over the dust-covered floor. Just as he was about to check out the objects lying all over the counter next to him, Mona pushed a large, heavy looking, leather-bound tome up to his leg.

"Look at this," she said as she wiped away some of the dust covering it, revealing a bright, unblemished, red-lacquered surface with gold inlaid patterns. "Isn't it cool? Have you ever seen strange writing like that?"

Aarvid picked up the large book and was surprised at how light it felt. Carefully, he placed it in his lap, and gently removed the cobwebs and remaining dust from its cover. When he studied the impressive black and red lacquered cover with golden patterns, he realized that Mona had been right. Those golden patterns were symbols and words of a language he was not familiar with.

"This book is in pretty good shape," he said, settling the book and moving around toward the light so he could get a better look and to get more comfortable. Without any further hesitation, he opened the book with Mona, stretched on her toes to get a better look, leaning in on his legs.

After what seemed like an eternity, Jenn reached the workbench located against the back wall of the room. She climbed feverishly, using fallen shelves and stray cobwebs to reach the top of the workbench. Just as she gained it, the dark little room was flooded by what at first appeared to be a blinding light. Looking across the cluttered counter top, she saw the reason for the change. Aarvid's slim, strong body was clearly outlined against the bright light of the now partially opened window. Fully extended, reaching up and out, he was pulling hard on the shutter until it twisted away with a groan.

A shuffling sound next to her made her turn around only to come face to face with Mona. Auburn hair framing her beautiful, soft features, she was looking at her brother with amazement. The close proximity of the youngsters, belying the real distance created by the magic realm, filled Jenn with an intense longing to again be part of a world with kids like these and people, real people. It had been too long, almost four hundred years.

From her perch on the workbench, she watched Aarvid, now seated on top of the workbench, as he carefully wiped the dust and cobwebs off the black and red, gold inscribed leather binding.

Protected from age and exposure by its own magic, the leather-bound book virtually glowed in the light entering from the partially opened window. She observed how the two youngsters were immediately completely absorbed in studying the magic tome. It was as if the book had cast a spell over them. Dismissing that idea as ridiculous, Jenn focused her mind to connect with Aarvid's.

Instantly, her mind was swept up by a powerful force that nearly overwhelmed her. Barely hanging on, she became aware of an amazing increase in the sensitivity of her senses. Colors and sounds seemed to have a life of their own, changing in intensity and hue as she tuned in on them. Never before had she experienced anything like it. It registered in her mind that it must be the magic. This magic sensitized her and raised her awareness to a level she had never experienced before—magic that was passed on to her mind from Aarvid's. Alarmed, she used all her efforts to refocus on the youngster who was avidly studying the pages, as he slowly turned them.

The intensified effort to reach out to his mind, hoping to protect him, resulted in a mental connection that made her feel as if she was inside his head. She experienced his fascination with and puzzlement at what was written on the pages as if they were her own. Everything he saw, she saw. Aghast at such a total intrusion, Jenn attempted to separate herself from the young man's mind, but was unable to do so.

She became aware that he was not just looking at the strange undecipherable language; he was reading and comprehending the magic written on the pages. Filled with dread, she found their combined minds slowly reading a magic spell that he was about to execute. At once, near panic engulfed her. Intuition derived from many years of experience in the magic realm told her that this spell did not feel right. Passing on the feeling of disquiet that she was experiencing to his mind, she was surprised to find that he had stopped and was turning to the next page. It struck her then how easy that had been and how close they had come to something potentially disastrous. There was no longer any doubt in her mind that this youngster had the ability. He could wield the magic and the magic was opening itself up to him, begging him to execute its spells.

Newly determined and feeling responsible for the situation they were dealing with, she decided to help guide him as well as she could.

Jenn was acutely aware of how little she knew about the powerful magic spells printed on the pages passing in front of their shared eyes. The impatience and inquisitiveness of his youthful mind pushed her to her mental limits trying to keep up with him. It required her total concentration to keep Aarvid from executing several other spells. She wondered if she had made a big mistake by getting the youngster in touch with the magic tome. Her own mind, increasingly unsure of itself, shouted at her, *You do not know the right spell or spells! How are you going to recognize it?*

It was quite clear to her now that some other, devious and powerful source of magic was at work here. It was testing his young mind—setting pitfalls that could be his undoing if in his eagerness he did not follow their combined instincts. The idea was sprouting in her mind, wondering if her role in this process was more than just coincidental. Not having much of a choice any more, Jenn hung on, amazed at the agility and speed of the juvenile mind she was attempting to guide.

Somewhere in her expanded consciousness it registered that they were soon to have company. She could sense their combined presence closing in on them, and there were more than just a few.

To Aarvid it was as if a filter had just been removed from in front of his eyes. He had just opened the large tome lying in his lap, when suddenly, as if magically, the strange script on the pages facing him seemed to settle and change. Not only did it appear larger and clearer, but he could grasp its meaning as well. Speaking the words written on the pages appeared to enhance his senses. First vague colors swirled over the words he spoke. The more he completed reading the words on the page, the more vivid became the colors as they slowly coalesced into colorful images—images that seemed to want to draw him in.

Thus far, whenever a spell he was reading got to the point where it was about to overwhelm him, he experienced a sensation of panic and stopped. He turned the pages one at a time, his young mind fascinated by the effects created by his spoken words. Heeding the feelings of disquiet, he stopped each time he sensed that the magic was ready to sweep him away. Aarvid recognized those feelings as coming from somewhere outside of himself. Yet, he trusted the source and was somewhat comforted by it since, in spite of his fascination, he was not quite sure what it was all about.

Just as he was exploring a particularly colorful and unusual page, he experienced a moment when his senses told him that he was no longer connected to that influence that had held him back; fleetingly it made him feel like he had been cast adrift. Apprehension washed over him. He knew he was losing control. Something strange was happening. A powerful influence was taking control of his mind.

Struggling to regain that control, feeling slightly panicked, he heard Mona's voice distorted and far distant speaking to him.

He could not respond. It was as if the outside world was shut off to him. The scripted words on the page he had been reading became alive as spoken words…words whispered, from a voice he could actually hear, a compelling voice that told him, "Aarvid, turn the page and read the next spell."

Helpless to do otherwise, he did so. As he did, the words slowly separated themselves from the page he was now reading and sinuously drifted toward him. When those words reached him, they transformed into colorful images that drew him in. From a great distance, he could hear his voice speaking the words, but in his mind he was no longer connected to the body that spoke those words.

As the spell approached its completion, more and more images swirled around him. Some were grotesque, others beautiful as they surrounded him, encircling him in soft, colorful bands until he was totally wrapped in a veil of colors.

Aarvid had stopped struggling. He had let himself be carried by the magic because his struggles had been futile, and somehow what he was experiencing had felt right. In the distance, far removed, he heard his voice speak the words, "Ihm Hibrayim Kush."

The rainbow of colors that had wrapped him up in their soft beauty started spinning. Since he was a part of them, he spun with them; first slowly, then more and more rapidly, until a sense of vertigo took hold of him. Instinctively, he tried to shut his eyes and reach out to grab hold of something, anything.

Aarvid found himself lying almost flat on his back, his eyes shut tight, and his hands clamped tight onto rough strands that were part of a strange, rough, and sinewy surface. It was what he saw with his eyes when he opened them that made him blink in disbelief.

Towering above him was a giant image of his younger sister's head, neck and shoulders. Fringed by her unruly auburn hair, Mona's huge, super-sized head had a frantic and confused look. The eyes, Mona's eyes, were desperately searching for something or someone. As the huge apparition opened its cavernous mouth, it let out a frightful, deafening, and high pitched, "AARVIIID! WHERE ARE YOU!?"

That loud scream, yelling his name jolted him out of his stupor. That giant apparition that had just shouted his name in desperation was in fact his sister.

While he struggled to his feet, a quick inventory of his surroundings revealed to him books, bottles, and other clutter the size of small and large buildings. Below his feet, he recognized the rough fibrous surface as the wooden surface of the workbench. Looking beyond it, he realized that he was still in the backroom. However, judging from the size of everything around him, something dramatic must have happened to him, something like having been reduced to the size of a tiny flea. Unwilling to belief what was happening to him, he whispered to himself, "Wow, this is some nightmare I'm having."

Repeating her high pitched scream, "AAAARVIIID, DON'T DO THIS!!" the giant version of Mona disappeared through a distant door. Once more, he was jolted by the realism of it.

A sudden loud rustling sound, followed by a thud, and a draft that almost knocked him off his feet made him spin around alarmed, just in time to see the final gilded pages of a huge, leather-bound tome flipping around and closing itself. Laying there among other smaller books and a clutter of giant sized bottles and other unrecognizable objects, Aarvid knew it as the book that had been the cause of all these changes. Realization set in; it struck him hard. Something extraordinary had indeed happened to him. Things were not the same!

"I am still in the backroom of the mill," he said softly, thinking out loud. "But, why is everything so strange, so huge?" he questioned, speaking a little louder.

"It is because you just entered into a world of magic, Aarvid." The voice that spoke was pleasant and comforting, but it had sadness to it. Troubled by the voice that seemed to know him, Aarvid turned to see a startlingly beautiful, young woman slowly step out from behind another of the building sized books.

Her roughly cut, short, blond hair seemed a perfect match to her athletic figure and the way she moved, while her startlingly blue eyes were an exclamation point to her fine features. Her presence only increased the impact his bizarre surroundings had on him.

"Who are you?" he asked incredulously. "I didn't know there was anyone else inside this room."

"Aarvid," she replied gently but with urgency, "there is no time to explain right now. Please trust me!" A concerned frown creased her perfect features. "I am Jenn," she continued, sounding slightly hurried, "I am somewhat responsible for your being here."

"But I…" Aarvid started to say.

"We'll go over that later," she interrupted. "Right now, we're in terrible danger!" Pausing for a moment to check their surroundings, she continued by suggesting, "Try to find something to defend yourself with. Anything pointed or sharp will do for now." Continuing with an urgency that was not to be denied she added, "Aarvid, please do it! Do it now!" As if to emphasize the fact that danger was imminent a threatening, rapidly increasing, buzzing sound was beginning to fill the room.

In spite of his unease, wanting to trust her, but unwilling to accept his own situation as dangerous, he insisted, "A weapon? What for?"

CHAPTER 4
PARTNERS IN FIGHT
AND FLIGHT

To Mona, the symbols on the pages of the large tome in her brother's lap were indecipherable. "What kind of language is that anyway?" she asked, not really expecting an answer.

Aarvid was studying each page carefully and mumbling words that made absolutely no sense to her. "As if he can understand what's written there," she expressed, thinking out loudly. At the same time, she was not feeling quite so sure because that was exactly what it was starting to look like.

When she took another close look at her brother, she started feeling very uncomfortable. She was puzzled by his intensity as he scrutinized each page. From the expression on his face, the mumbled words and phrases that sounded like gibberish to her appeared to have real meaning to him.

To Mona it seemed that Aarvid had drifted away from her. He appeared to have forgotten that she was there. It was as if he was in a trance, or trapped in some sort of spell. How could that be?

An intense stab of fear and worry coursed through her. Something was very wrong here. Desperate to snap him out of his trance-like state, she shook his legs. He did not appear to notice and continued mumbling. Barely able to speak from anxiety, she moaned, "Aarvid, what are you doing? What are you saying?"

Aarvid's face had become pale. He appeared lost in concentration, yet his eyes had lost their focus while his mouth continued mumbling those unrecognizable words. Mona had just decided to take the book out of his slightly trembling hands, when she heard him raise his voice and slowly pronounce what sounded like, "Ihm Hibrayim Khush."

Confused, she stumbled up against the edge of the now unoccupied workbench. Just a moment ago she had anxiously pushed up against his legs, her hands overlapping his in preparation for a struggle to remove the book from his grasp. Now, there was not a trace of her brother and she was left holding the huge tome. This could not be happening! Bewildered she looked around the small room. Her mind racing to repeat the events that had just transpired, she gently placed the large book on the workbench.

When it hit her that her brother had really just disappeared into thin air, panic overtook her. "Aarvid! Where are you!" she screamed, frantic with fear. When all remained totally silent, except for the slight scraping noise of that branch outside the window, she lost all composure. Stifling sobs, she ran to the door leading out of the room, shouting one final, "Aarvid, don't do this!!"

She failed to notice the angry buzzing noises that were starting to enter the little room through the open window, as she ran off into the dark interior of the mill.

Ever since their narrow escape from death in 1303, Kirchner had been in command of the Praetorian Guards assigned to Cardinal Mephistopheles while in the magic realm. Since that time not only had his 6'6" frame more than doubled in girth, he had developed into a cruel, ruthless executioner always assigned the toughest, most difficult jobs. He was proud of his reputation for brutal cruelty. He considered his designated targets as prey, almost never bothering to spare lives. "Chlet theyer boones shake for feayer," he loved to say in his guttural growl.

Today his mood was even fouler than it usually was. Assignments like this were regularly reserved for his assistant Crawitz. What made him even angrier was the fact that he was forced to reach his target on the back of this yellowjacket. His fear of heights was not helped out by the fact that his massive body had not much more to hang on to except for a couple of tiny spikes protruding from the insect's sleek back, nor was it diminished by the creature's propensity to show of its flying prowess by rapid accelerations and diving for its target at dizzying speeds.

Holding on for all his might, he grumbled, "Roust mich from mine trink. Sjust for shome little bratt and a girrel. Phah!" Trying to distract himself from his discomfort, he continued, "Firsht, Ich wiel shpank zem both; shpank zem real goohd!" That thought excited him and made him forget somewhat the height at which they were flying. Getting more into it, and forgetting his orders not to kill, he continued, "Maybe Ich wiel sjust haf shom fun wieth zem firsht. Zen, Ich wiel cut zem uop and feed zem to ze antsh." The anticipation made him feel almost his usual self.

The rapidly approaching outline of the windmill indicated they were nearing their target. Turning to his assistant, Commander Crawitz, flying yet another yellowjacket nearby, he shouted, "Hey, Crawitz, schnap to it chou dull-brained sjon of a gwhore!"

It had its intended effect as Crawitz turned a bright shade of pink while keeping his attention fixed on their target. His mentally conveyed response was a terse, *Your orders?*

Kirchner decided not to push his second in command any further. He felt better already knowing they were rapidly nearing their target. This time, using mental telepathy, the appropriate manner for issuing orders, his aggressively transmitted commands were, *Ich wiel chandle zies lichle situachion. Chou and chour schwad schtay up hier and ensjoy chourschelves on zies chdammed beaschts. Warn mich if anything unuushual happench!*

Kirchner's small contingent containing roughly a dozen armored and mounted guards buzzed the perimeter of the old structure twice before deciding to enter through the small opening in the shuttered window out in the back. Before entering, he gave his troops their final instructions by mentally conveying, *Ich wiel take care of ze young manch. Joachim und Manfred, chou are with mich. Everybody elsch, go and discharm the girrel. Put a markchen on her schweet body and chou wiel anschwer to mich! She ist mine! Unterschtand?* The last couple of orders were bitten off aggressively.

With those final instructions the heavily armored troop passed through the opened window into the small backroom of the old windmill.

The creature landed between Jenn and himself. In spite of its huge, bulky appearance, Aarvid recognized it as a very large man covered in armor made from discarded pieces of insect exoskeleton. His powerful, long arms seemed to end in jagged claws, one of which was resting on the hilt of a huge broadsword hanging from his hip. For one short moment the strange warrior took in the startled form of Jenn. Then slowly, the armor-clad giant turned around to face Aarvid. From beneath bushy eyebrows two intensely cruel, steel-blue eyes fixed themselves on his trembling body.

The rough, age-worn features were partially hidden by a short, unkempt beard. After a moment of sizing up the slim eleven-year-old wearing nothing but a pair of shorts, a wide grin split the tangled growth underneath the large knobby nose, revealing two rows of blackened, rotting teeth; a low chuckling, grumbling noise escaped his cavernous maw as he started toward Aarvid.

Never before in his young life had Aarvid experienced such mind-numbing fear as that caused by those cruel, blue eyes. This was only increased by the disorienting appearance of vivid pictures in his mind of his own bloodied body being subjected to unthinkable perversions and abuse, while strange guttural and menacing words rang through his head.

Unaware of his body's movements, feeling like helpless prey about to be snatched up and torn to pieces, he stumbled backward and tripped. As he felt himself falling, he thought he recognized the shiny golden edged pages of the now building-sized magic tome. When he hit the ground with his body, his hand struck something hard protruding from the binding of the tome. The painful sting shattered the web of fear that had trapped him. Instantly, awareness flooded his mind that the visions were not his own, but were in fact projected by the huge warrior he faced. That insight was followed by a determination to defend himself; he'd made up his mind, he would rather die than submit to the debased treatment his nemesis had in mind for him.

Gathering himself, ready to scramble up before the slowly advancing warrior could reach him, he mumbled, "Holy B-Jeepers! I am going to need some sort of weapon. Where…?" He never finished the question because while scrambling to get of the ground, his right hand had grabbed the hard object that protruded from the binding of the magic tome. When he pulled, it came free nestling nicely in his hand.

Squatting low, with the magic tome behind his back, Aarvid brought up his hand with what he hoped would be some sort of object that would keep his opponent away from him long enough to make a speedy get-away. What caught his eye was the glitter of blue steel protruding from his hand.

For a moment he caught his breath. *A sword! Where had that come from?* It was indeed a formidable weapon for someone his size. As he moved it back and forth in front of him, its straight, keen double edges sparkled in the light.

There was no more time to dwell on it, because the huge apparition had drawn its own monstrous broad-sword and continued to advance on him. With its rumbling chuckle indicating amusement, a deep gravely voice uttered, "Scho shou found chourschelf a tiny shtinger, eh?"

Still scared out of his wits, but somewhat buoyed by his pointed acquisition, Aarvid asked in a quavering voice, "Who are you and what do you wa…?"

Once again, he did not finish the question, because a flash of yellow and black, buzzing noisily had just deposited another armored warrior to the right of the huge caricature of a human he had been addressing. Overhead, the buzzing of yellowjackets continued indicating the arrival of more warriors. The slight noise of heavy breathing to his left, slightly out of his field of vision, told him that another opponent had just arrived on the scene. The new arrivals did not advance and were apparently waiting for orders from his first opponent.

"Chwhy don't chou drop chour lichle knife, boyh." Spoken in a guttural heavy accent, its tone so menacing, it sent a shiver down Aarvid's spine. "If shou do, Ich wiel nicht hurt shou much!" As the armored warrior spoke this time, he pointed his broad sword in the direction of Aarvid's chest. In his cold blue eyes Aarvid recognized a flicker of cruel hunger as once again his mind received an onslaught of the visions that had tormented him earlier. This time Aarvid was prepared and with determination shut his mind to the intrusions and threw them back at his opponent. He was rewarded momentarily by a slight widening of the ice-blue eyes and what looked like a brief flash of surprise by the bushy eyebrows that overhung them. Unfortunately for him, that seemed to have decided it for the huge warrior. Waving his large weapon he gave a few guttural commands to the other two warriors who had been standing off. Slowly, weapons raised and prepared to strike they advanced on Aarvid as well.

With time running out, Aarvid quickly took in his surroundings. To his back was the building sized magic tome. Not too far away, slightly off to his left he knew would be the chasm that lay beyond the edge of the workbench. The clutter of large and small objects prevented him from seeing too far. Yet, those objects might provide him opportunity to duck behind if even for just a second or two.

Beyond the three warriors closing in on him, the shouting and cursing of a fight could already be heard. Intuitively he knew that Jenn would give a good accounting of herself. However, from the sound of the many voices, he feared that she would soon be overwhelmed.

Remembering the images of abuse intended for him, his mind steeled itself in grim determination. Suddenly, in a flash, the memory of his lessons in Karate and his more advanced lessons using Kendo came back to him; recalling the feel of the bamboo "Kendo Shinai" practice sword in his hands brought with it a calming, focusing of the mind. *Remember, focus yourself. Become one with your weapon. To become a warrior you must think like one. Quickness will overcome power,* the memories whispered in his mind.

Crouching low, he experienced a moment of lightheadedness and felt surprised by the adrenalin rush that overtook him next, sweeping away any residue of fear. He hardly heard the guttural insults meant to strike fear into his soul.

"Phah! Shou zink shou can do hurt with shour lichle schtinger, lichle boyh? Hah! Shou look more like a schweet lichle girrel!" With those utterances the huge bearded warrior raised his sword. It was almost as long as Aarvid was tall. After a short hesitation, the blade started its sweeping, downward arc.

It seemed like everything moved in slow motion while in a slight haze. It was as if he could see all around him. His increased awareness took in the powerful arc of the large sword as it circled in on him from his left. Instinctively, almost casually, he prepared his body for the parry, moving his feet, shifting his weight, and turning his own weapon to intercept it.

With a loud clang the weapons met just inches from his face. Blue sparks escaped from the bright metal of his sword and jumped onto the oversized broadsword wielded by his giant attacker.

Commander Kirchner, looking at the slender, nearly naked pre-teen holding in front of him a contemptibly puny weapon, intended to waste no more time. His head still throbbing from the mental whip lashing he had received, compliments of this child, he prepared to finish it with one single blow. The sooner this was finished, the sooner the fun he had promised himself could begin.

Lifting his weapon and placing as much force behind it as he could muster, he brought it down in an arc, flat side leading toward the youth's head. He was surprised by the lack of fear in the youngster's eyes, next by the grace and fluid quickness of his movements. Kirchner's biggest surprise was the unexpected way his own stroke, executed with brutish strength, was stopped. It was as if he had struck a solid metal pole; shockwaves rattled his brain and hurt his rotting teeth. But worse, the blue lightning that traveled up his sword cramped his sword-hand with such pain, he almost dropped his weapon. Not willing to let on to his companions how surprising and painful this first exchange had been, he blustered, "Scho shou want to play, ehh?"

Not giving himself time to reflect on what just happened, Aarvid focused inward, reminding him, *I've got to go on the offensive, there's three of them. I'm not going to become their plaything! Use quickness and do the unexpected.*
Once more he experienced that slight feeling of dizziness, with it once again came the sensation that time had slowed down and his senses were primed. It was time to attack.

To the already bloodied rat-faced creature who was trying to sneak up on the young boy, it seemed that one moment the child had been fairly immobile, just shuffling his feet and parrying the powerful blow dealt by Kirchner; the next he had been a blur spinning away from the two warriors. After a forward roll the child instantly gained his feet and was now face to face with him. The rat-faced creature knew it was its turn to strike; excited by the prospect of finishing the job that the mighty Her Kirchner had not been able to complete, it brought its weapon to bear in a deadly arc aimed for the shoulders and head of the boy.

For a moment Aarvid was taken aback by the half gnome, half human apparition with rat-like features. In his mind he heard Jenn urging him on, warning him of the terrible things that could be awaiting them. For just an instant, he was amazed by this ability to communicate mentally. While he dove under the arc of the gnome's stroke, he used that ability to respond to her. *Hang in there, Jenn, I'll be there to help in just a few moments.* Aarvid's dive brought him behind his attacker; rolling to his feet, maintaining his low crouch, he slashed his own weapon across the back of its heels. With a yammering howl the gnome-like rat face collapsed to the ground, reaching for its ankles.

When Aarvid prepared for his next move, there was a loud cry coming from where Jenn was engaging her attackers. A quick glance in that direction revealed several of her attackers down and bloodied. However, the circle of remaining warriors seemed to be pressing in on her and he could clearly sense her desperation. It was not difficult to guess that it would be only a matter of time before she would be overwhelmed by the sheer number of her opponents. He knew that he had no other option but to engage his two remaining opponents. He had to find a way to render them harmless so that he could help Jenn.

In his mind's eye he could see his next move. Almost sprinting at his opponents, he faked toward the smaller of the two warriors who were blocking his path and had their weapons raised in anticipation.

Kirchner no longer felt the way he had entering this engagement. His brain still throbbed and he was confused by the painful intensity of his first contact with his child-like opponent. However, any doubt he had that he faced a more than worthy foe had been erased by the ease with which the child had dispatched the gnome-like mercenary whose earlier task had been to corner Jenn inside the mill. Thoughts of fun and sadistic pleasure were replaced by the bur of an upwelling of fear. He had never failed an assignment given to him. Would he be able to pull this off? If only he did not feel so unsteady from drinking too much. Gritting his painful teeth, he spat out to his companion, "Chou catch chim going shour gway, chou kill him!" In a menacing growl he added, "Failch and chou dieh!"

A couple of steps away from his apparent target, Aarvid suddenly changed direction. Remembering his martial arts training, he launched himself, body spinning in mid-air, at the gap between the two armored men hoping that they would not use their weapons to intercept him for fear of hitting one another.

Aarvid was astounded by the ease with which he executed the move and with the incredible height of his leap. In the past, he had executed many summersaults and always prided himself on not using his hands, but this felt totally different; it was almost as if he could fly.

With his head rotated downward, toward the ground, he saw the giant warrior make a belated move to intercept him. The tip of the sword just barely missed him. However, the unbridled force behind the swing carried it downward, completing its arc by crashing into the shoulder of the smaller warrior, severing his arm.

Landing neatly on his feet, Aarvid immediately turned to face his foes. He was momentarily taken aback by the sight of the severed arm lying in a puddle of blood. With time still moving in slow motion, he watched as the injured warrior crumpled slowly to the floor. Behind him the exuberance of the shouts coming from the direction where Jenn was engaged told him that time was running out for her.

Aarvid pressed the attack immediately. Taking advantage of his foe's temporary confusion, he quickly rolled under the other's guard. Instantly, in a low crouch, he delivered a quick blow with his sword to the back of the man's knee. With a crunch his weapon passed through armor into bone, and…was stuck.

Still standing, bellowing from pain with a force that could have brought down the walls of the small room, the huge warrior swung his own weapon down toward Aarvid.

Seeing the huge sword come arching down on him, he quickly let go of his own weapon, pivoted and rolled to the warrior's other side. Balancing himself on his hands, using all the force his frail young body could muster, he executed a two-footed kick aimed at the side of the warrior's other knee.

The sound of cracking bone was followed by a renewed ear-splitting howl from the frustrated and badly injured warrior. Slowly, the giant body toppled over and landed face down on top of the already prostrate form of the other warrior.

Quickly, Aarvid jumped over the slumped form to retrieve his own weapon and to join Jenn.

Almost immediately after the huge warrior she recognized as Kirchner, commander of the pack that was about to engage them, turned toward Aarvid, Jenn found herself being surrounded by other warriors. Each was well armed, wearing armor made of insect skeletons and of a size that made her seem diminutive and defenseless.

Holding her own weapon menacingly in front of her, she tried to give herself as much space as possible by darting back and forth inside the circle formed by her attackers. However, no matter how quickly she moved, she found herself moving in constantly smaller and smaller circles.

"Give it up, girl." The command was spoken by a large rotund warrior. His hairy navel, protruding from under the armor, his only unprotected body part. Jenn could not make out his features from behind the insect-like mask. However, the weapon he wielded, a sword roughly half the length of her own body, indicated formidable strength.

"It's not going to be that easy!" she spat back angrily. Jenn knew that she was physically overmatched. There was no turning around at this point. She was committed, even if it meant dying. Aware of her quandary, she was nevertheless sick with worry about Aarvid. What would happen to him if she failed to extricate herself and him out of this somehow?

"Be careful! She's quick and dangerous!" Jenn recognized the speaker, the larger of the two mercenary scouts that had cornered her earlier. She also noticed the disdain his warning received from the others circling her.

The voice of the leader had a dangerous edge to it as he urged, "Girl, you don't mean anything to me. Spare yourself pain or worse! I'll give my word. You'll go free when this thing is over, if you give it up NOW!"

Jenn recognized the lie. She had been in the magic realm long enough to be able to get past his clumsy effort to hide his thoughts from her. Besides, she picked up plenty of hints of what was in store for her from the others surrounding her.

Allowing her a few moments to make a decision, the leader barked out orders to the group. Jenn chose that moment to attack. Driving her pointed weapon at his unprotected naval, she pounced on the unprepared warrior, felling him. Next, she furiously attacked the nearest warrior, seriously wounding him as well. Rushing to the other side of her circle of enemies, she attacked again, creating confusion in her foes, yet she continued to be surrounded. There were just too many of them.

She used the little interlude gained from her sudden attack to mentally connect with Aarvid. *Aarvid! Fight them! Do not let them take you! They will do horrible things to you!*

His mentally conveyed response gave her renewed hope and with it energy to keep going. Aarvid was managing his situation. She had no time to figure how; right now it was enough to know that he was.

Like a whirling dervish, inflicting pain and injury wherever her quick strokes struck home, Jenn attempted to keep her attackers off balance. She could sense that she would not be able to keep this pace up much longer.

Jenn was desperately in need for a break. Her legs were starting to cramp up. She could barely lift her sword to defend herself, never mind inflicting harm. Gasping for air, while continuing her desperate defense, she was as surprised as her attackers.

The ear splitting, growling, guttural howl coming from one of Aarvid's attackers brought all of her opponents up short and seemed to be a serious distraction. "That's Kirchner. He's been hurt!" she heard one say. "How could that be?" another blurted out. "There must be others attacking him," was another's comment.

"You coward!" The words were spat out by a giant of a man. A vicious scar disfigured what at one time must have been a face. Eyes dark and hateful, a discolored hole of a mouth spat out, "Get yourselves back to fighting the little witch, you spineless, good for nothing sons of a brothel!"

Her opponents, remembering their orders, immediately resumed pressing in on her. Recognizing that she had used up most of her energy, they shouted loudly in an attempt to animate one another. It seemed to work, because they could feel that they were closing in on her and the quick movements that had previously effectively kept them at a distance were slowly becoming more and more sluggish. Just when they thought that they were about to finish her off…swoosh…a lithe, nearly naked body hurtled through the air.

Whooping out a fierce fight cry, "Haaiiyah!" and shouting an encouraging, "Hang in there, Jenn!" the young slender boy, his gleaming sword raised above his head, landed squarely on the shoulders of the large, scar-faced warrior.

Once again, with time moving as though through molasses and his senses peaked, Aarvid found himself astride the warrior he had identified as the leader of the pack that surrounded Jenn. Hoping to cut off circulation to the warrior's brain, he squeezed his legs firmly on either side of the brute's thick neck. When the warrior raised his sword to strike at him, Aarvid brought down his own weapon, lopping off the end of the arm holding on to the sword. Between his legs he could see the bulging veins on the purple, hatred filled, scarred face; the red-rimmed eyes nearly popped out of their eye sockets as they rolled upward, attempting to catch a glimpse of him.

In spite of his injuries and discomfort, the warrior continued his struggles to rid himself of the pesky child. When next the other arm, covered in armor reached up for him, Aarvid reflexively ducked forward avoiding the lumber-like appendage. While falling forward, as he passed the now purple face, he stabbed his own sword down at the warrior's chest. With the crunching sound of armor, the blade entered.

Aarvid landed feet first and immediately moved to cover Jenn's backside.

Once more the warriors were distracted from pressing their attack on Jenn. The attack cry uttered by the child as it flew through the air to land on Scar-Face's shoulders had seemed amusing at first. What followed, confused them more than a little; watching the huge warrior, his right arm a bloody stump, tilt forward slowly and crumple to the ground, was enough to back most of them away from the melee, away from this dangerous pair.

With most of her attackers now more concerned with keeping themselves at a safe distance from her stabs and slashes, Jenn knew that the tide had turned and with it their chances for survival. Feeling Aarvid's slender body pressed against her back comforted her immensely. It was as if she had just been relieved of an incredible burden. Not allowing herself to become emotional and knowing that their situation was far from resolved, she checked his condition by asking, "Are you hurt?"

Slightly out of breath, gently probing, he responded, "I'm OK. Are you?"

Jenn was both surprised and pleased with the tone of his answer and his concern for her. Speaking softly and still trying to catch her breath, she pressed on, "Thank you, Aarvid...I am fine...Just a scratch or two...Nothing serious...Listen! We need to get away from here before they regroup!...Are you ready?"

Casually trusting, he replied, "Sure! Where to?"

"You'll see. Just follow my lead," she responded, in a hurry to escape their predicament before their enemies got a chance to regroup.

"We'll attack side by side. Ready?" Without waiting for an answer, she exhorted, "GO!" Jenn led their charge at a small group of warriors. Confused and leaderless, their opponents scattered at their approach.

It appeared that their way toward escape was free.

Firmly grasping Aarvid by the arm that held his sword, she pointed her own weapon at rope-like remains of an old spider web draped over the far corner of the cluttered workbench.

"Aarvid, once we reach those—" She was interrupted by the appearance of a bulky, powerful built, human-like creature, with a snout-like face. It stepped out from behind one of the large objects to block their path.

Aarvid had never met the creature before. However, Jenn and the brute seemed to know one another. While an ugly gash still oozed blood along the side of its barrel chest, it croaked, "You'll not be rid of me as easy this time, little lady," and came charging at them.

Looking askance at Jenn, Aarvid received a quick, reassuring wink, followed by a nod directed toward the left side of the charging brute, immediately followed by another nod at the rope-like web that hung down over the far edge of the workbench.

Just before the rapidly approaching creature got within striking distance with its sword, she gave him a quick shove. Instantly Aarvid dipped and scurried to the left past the blur of the bulky form, while Jenn, matching him in quickness, took off to its right.

While the creature bellowed in frustration, Jenn and Aarvid ran on toward the remains of an old spider web.

"Watch me! Do what I do!" With that she leaped at one of the old strands, wrapped her legs around it, and, while holding on with one hand, used the other to slash free its lower end.

Slowly the strand pulled itself free and started its arching swing toward some boards leaning at an angle against the side wall.

Aarvid did not need any urging. Behind him he heard shouts indicating the beginning of pursuit. Quickly, he jumped onto another strand and soon was swinging through the air, heading toward the boards.

Below him, he could see Jenn who had switched over to another of the rope-like strands in mid-air, and was now sliding down it toward the slanted boards.

Aarvid, not having a place to stash his sword, and not used to swinging one-handed from ropes, suddenly realized that he had swung past the closest point to the slanted boards. When the strand reversed its swing, he quickly judged its nearest point of passage over the boards and let go.

His off-balanced landing on the slanted surface forced him to make a couple of forward rolls that quickly gathered momentum. Unintentionally, wanting to regain some control, he focused his mind, planning his next move. For just a fleeting moment he had a wishful vision of sliding down a long, snowy ramp on a sled. Immediately, it was followed by a slight tickle in his head as time slowed.

As if in slow motion, yet rolling downhill out of control, Aarvid whipped his body outward and slapped his feet down on the slanted, dusty surface. He quickly realized that, even with his feet under him, he was still accelerating down the ramp. As a matter of fact, he was moving so fast, he had the sensation he was literally flying down the sloped surface. A bump on the ramp sent him airborne; bending down and tucking in his legs for balance, he reached down with his free hand to an object folded around his feet. Moments later, when he landed on the slanted board again, he found himself hanging on for his life to…a piece of paper. Acting as a sled on the dirt-coated surface, it rapidly deposited him into the thick layer of dust covering the floor. For a moment the explosion of dust and motes rendered everything invisible.

Coughing from the dust that quickly settled all around him, Aarvid looked up the ramp where Jenn, still clinging to a strand of webbing, was running down the steep slope. With her free hand waving toward a section of the wall, she shouted, "Aarvid, go through that crack in the wall behind you. I will be right behind you!"

To Aarvid, everything around him was unfamiliar and he hesitated. Looking back at Jenn, he decided that he was not ready to travel this strange world by himself. He had found a companion he trusted and felt comfortable with, one who might guide him through this strange ordeal. He did not want to take any chance at losing her, so he was not going to let her out of his sight.

Instead, he attempted to brush some of the dust off himself. It was then that he noticed he was still holding his weapon. Startled, he realized it was smeared with blood. In the next instance it hit him, the impact of the violence of which he had been a part. This was not a dream, he knew better. The beings he had fought, maimed, and killed had been real. For a few moments, his legs felt rubbery, his stomach felt weak, and he started to shake. Then, Jenn stood in front of him and the moment passed.

"Are you OK?" she managed, gulping air. "You look a little pale underneath all that dirt." Snickering, she added lightly, "If you could have seen yourself. I have never seen anyone going down such a ramp quite that way. Are you sure you're not from some circus?" Still chuckling, while she brushed off the flakey dust motes stuck to his body, "You are a sight. Look at your face and body. You're all fuzzy and streaked with grime."

Self conscious of his lack of clothing, he turned slightly away from her with a, "I'm all right, Jenn."

At that moment he heard sounds of pursuit from on top of the workbench and realized that they should have been running, making their way through that hole in the wall. He knew that Jenn had taken the time to allow him to settle down. Quickly he brushed at the largest pieces of dirt clinging to his legs and started for the wall, asking, "Is it over there?"

Pointing in the direction they were to head, she responded, "Yes, but let me lead. I know the way and I will know where they may be laying other traps for us." As they started for the wall, she reassuringly touched his shoulder and added, "Aarvid, actually I am glad you waited for me."

Jogging as fast as the thick layer of dirt covering the floor allowed them to, they slogged over and around obstacles toward the crack in the wall that separated the backroom from the central portion of the old mill.

Commander Crawitz could not believe what he was hearing; the messenger had decided to deliver the report in person, to be certain that all the details would be clear.

"So, please repeat once more what you observed," he ordered tersely.

"Commander, while I circled overhead, I saw the most incredible battle. Never before have I seen anything like this. This child! It must have been a demon spawn! Suddenly, out of nowhere, this nearly naked child drew out a weapon that sparked bolts of blue lightning. Commander, this demon child—"

"Just stick to the facts as you saw them," Crawitz interrupted. "Start again, and this time from the beginning!"

"Uhh...well." Composing himself, the messenger

swallowed. Then, he resumed, "Nothing seemed out of the ordinary at first. The girl and the child were both surprised by Commander Kirchner's landing. The child even stumbled and fell down, looking just like all the others that had to face Commander Kirchner. Then, suddenly, all hell broke loose. With that weapon he obtained out of nowhere, his naked body was spinning and flying through the air like nothing I've ever seen. All the while that little sword was giving off sparks of blue fire. Amazingly, seemingly without much effort, the child dispatched the Commander and two others. Then, with that sword still sparking bolts of blue lightning, he joined the fighting around the girl. In a matter of seconds, those two injured or killed over half of the squad."

"Where were they when you left the area?"

"Commander, they appeared to be headed toward the large central room."

"Very well," was the thoughtful response. Then, making up his mind, he instructed, "I am placing you in command. Have half of my remaining men take up positions inside the old mill and return with the remainder to the battle scene. Leave a couple of the healers to help the wounded. Instruct all able men to start pursuit immediately. They must establish and maintain contact at all cost. If this is not done, you will all answer to the wrath of the mages!"

CHAPTER 5
UNPLEASANT
TRUTHS

The cave was a bustle of large shiny dark bodies. The glow of fungi and molds growing on the walls and low ceiling produced a faint phosphorescent light, sufficient to reveal giant ants working their underground gardens. On the far end of the long enclosure, just around a bend in the cave, a brighter, magically created light illuminated the two powerful mages of the magic realm where they listened to the report presented by Commander Crawitz.

The Black Mage's concern and unhappiness was self evident by the manner in which he slowly paced back and forth in front of the commander; the scowl on his face was half masked by the hand that continued to stroke his angular chin.

Dressed in his customary blood red gown, the reclining form of Cardinal Mephistopheles silently took in the news. He appeared totally relaxed; his huge body, draped over a throne-like seat formed by roots protruding from the wall of the cave, seemed unaffected except for the more violent twitching of his tail-like appendage, and the red hot rage in the burning eyes.

"So, you believe that your remaining guards have them trapped inside the old mill?" The Cardinal's voice was a dry hiss of barely suppressed anger.

"The last telepathic report I received indicated that was the case, Your Excellency," was the subdued answer.

"And how many dead?" The black mage had stopped his pacing and looked at Crawitz, waiting for the answer.

"Three, definitely. There is some question if even the rapid healing in our realm will save two of the worst injured," he replied, continuing to stand at attention.

"Kirchner?" The question was terse and unemotional.

"I believe he will recover physically, Your Grace."

The emphasis on "physical" provided David a clue where the real concern was concerning Commander Kirchner.

"He deserved what he got," David said as he prepared to dismiss Crawitz. Suddenly remembering, his wave of dismissal turned into the raised hand that demands attention. Emphasizing each word, he added, "I want NO harm to come to the boy! Try to trap them in one place if possible until I can deal with them personally." Holding Crawitz's attention with his intense stare, he waited until the commander nodded his understanding before dismissing him and turning his attention toward the reclining form of the Cardinal.

From within the impenetrable darkness of his deep cowl, his low rumbling voice issued from beneath two feral, yellow eyes, "Why go easy on the whelp, David? Hasn't he caused enough trouble already?…And the girl?…May God have mercy on her when we do catch her!" There was no mistaking his agitation. Only his deep seated respect for his partner, particularly

David's far superior abilities to wield the magic, kept him from exploding into one of his well known temper tantrums.

When David did not answer as quickly as he liked, he continued while his appendage swished more excitedly, "You do realize the severity of the situation if the young man is allowed to discover his powers in this realm? Do you, David?"

Nodding to himself, as if confirming some suspicion, David replied absentmindedly, "I am not sure that I can do much, other than slow him down. He has given ample proof of his untested abilities already. If provoked, he will only grow stronger and more dangerous to us."

While he spoke he removed a folded piece of paper from his pocket. Unfolding it he explained, "I do not know why I always kept a copy of this handy someplace. Something made me remember that I had it. Actually, you also might remember, since this was one of several pieces that I was able to translate from the magic tome when we first discovered it. In the nearly eight hundred years since, I have not been able to decipher one single additional page."

Holding it to the light he read:

"We Shamans have worked for more than 14 cycles of the moon to complete the magic contained in these scrolls. By combining our knowledge, we have created a magic with the means to perform lasting magical feats in as many ways as there are colors in the rainbow.

"To make certain that our work will perform true to its destiny, we have created guardian spells that will prevent any future Shaman from abusing the power held within these scrolls, while at the same time insuring that these writings will continue their existence."

After a short pause and a quick look to insure he had the full attention of his partner, he continued, "The rest of the piece is a critical description of the type of magic contained in the tome.

Unfortunately, the symbolism used here was a little more cryptic and open to several interpretations. The following were the most important pieces of that description and the way I translated it:

"...as the 15 created this, a lasting monument,
A magic spell so pure its fabric unseen,
Its magic never fading, changing in appearance,
Blending itself with customs, changed over time.
Wielded not by hunger for power.
A choice of master made by the magic that serves,
Yielding knowledge grudgingly,
Until its wielder be the innocent(s),
Mind(s) wise to the charge.
For the good of all."

Following a deep breath, his face screwed up with the effort to make the correct conclusion, David lectured on, "These passages, at least some of them, seem to indicate that the tome has the ability to choose who wields the magic. Maybe it even manipulates events to cause this to happen. It may have happened already!...The innocent(s)...The young boy and his sister?"

Rising to tower over his dark-cloaked companion, the bulky form of the cardinal growled, "That makes it even more crucial that we recover the book; recover it before it can do any more harm. There is no way on God's earth that this child could have absorbed all of its content in the short time he had before the guards got to them. So far, his sister has displayed no magical talents."

Nodding acquiescence, his face still screwed, the Black Mage mumbled, "Yes! At least we'll find out if it is still there, accessible to us."

Before she realized it, Mona was stumbling into the bright light outside the old mill. For a moment she stood there taking in the feel of the hazy, hot late summer day that had started out with such promise. Earlier, she had stood there with her brother before the mysterious door, anxious and yet excited by a sense of adventure. Now, she felt alone, frightened and confused. Aarvid, her best friend, her brother, was stuck in there somewhere; she was sure of it. He was in some sort of trouble. What was she to do?

Anke and Wim had started for the mill when they first heard Mona's shrill shouts for her brother. Apprehensive, and not certain of themselves, they had stumbled along the pond toward the half-open door of the old structure. To them it looked more impressive and foreboding than ever, the stories of it being haunted, becoming more real as they came closer to it. When they saw Mona emerge from the door, dirt-streaked and teary-eyed, they temporarily forgot their apprehensions and rushed over to her.

The sight of her friends coming toward her through the knee-high weeds, sent Mona running to them. The feel of Anke's reassuring hug, as she buried her face in Anke's chest, released her pent-up anxieties and with it uncontrolled sobs. She could feel Anke drape a towel around her and Wim empathetically embracing them both.

As her own emotions drained away with the sobs, a surge of fear welled up in her. It felt different; it was a troubled fear, a fear for what might be happening to her brother. Along with it, a growing sense of urgency told her she had to do something. Aarvid needed her help.

As if from a distance, she could hear Anke's anxious and

repeated questions, "Mona, tell me where is Aarvid? Please, tell me what happened in there."

Interrupted by an occasional sob and uncontrolled tears that blurred her vision, Mona blurted out, "I don't know!...I was holding him...and then...he just disappeared!"

"Let's go inside and look for him," suggested Wim, sounding more sure than he felt.

"No! We have to get help! I'm too scared to go inside there again!" Mona's shrill response conveyed her fears to her friends. It drained away any desire they had to enter the forbidden-looking structure.

When Mona urged them to accompany her home, to get her mom, they quickly agreed.

"Mom!...Mom!" Gemma recognized the shrill, hysterical shouts as Mona's. Alarmed, she ran out the kitchen door. Mona was just then approaching at a tired run, down the road where it sloped down from the bridge that crossed the canal; her friends, looking equally haggard, following close behind. When Gemma realized that Aarvid was not with them, a knot formed in the pit of her stomach. Running to meet her daughter, her voice unable to conceal her panic, she shouted, "Honey, what's wrong? Where is your brother?"

They met just outside the gate; Mona, her grimy, sweat-and-tear-streaked face a grimace of anxiety, uttered a single desperation-filled, "Mom," before burying her face in her mother's dress.

Gemma tenderly cuddled her sobbing daughter, looking askance at her two friends who stood pale faced, and with tears filling their eyes, a few paces back. Neither Anke nor Wim spoke, choosing to let Mona do the talking.

Clinging to her mother as they walked back to the house,

with sobs racking her anew, Mona told her tale of how she and Aarvid had gone into the old windmill, how they had found the small backroom and Aarvid's unusual fascination with a book before he disappeared... "One moment, I was holding onto his legs trying to get a look, the next he was just gone," she finished, wiping the tears out of her eyes with the back of her hands.

Looking for anything else that might be helpful, Gemma looked toward Anke and Wim. Anke, sitting down, while Wim stood forlornly in the door, both shook their heads in response to the question in her eyes. After a moment, Anke added softly, "We did not go in with them. But we saw both Aarvid and Mona go inside. Only Mona came back out. She was upset and in tears, and said that Aarvid had disappeared."

Hugging her distraught daughter, even as Anke was speaking, Gemma's mind went over the events she had been told. She could not believe what she was hearing. *Aarvid disappear?* she asked herself. *That is just so not like him...He'd never leave his little sister...Would he?...But then, where is he?...What could possibly have happened to him?*

Seated in one of the kitchen chairs, she looked down at the slight figure of her daughter huddled in her lap, her body shaking with each sob, hugging her tightly as if for reassurance. Gemma could feel desperation starting to build up inside of her; she put it down—she could not allow the panic to sweep her wits away. She had to believe that what she was told was essentially true. She trusted her daughter; even more, she trusted Aarvid. She told herself, *There has to be another explanation...Something strange must have happened...But, what?*

After notifying the local constable and arranging to meet at the mill, Gemma gave Mona a dry shirt to wear over her bathing suit and prepared to return to the old windmill. Gemma, her emotions just barely in check, thanked Anke and Wim and sent them home.

During the fairly long walk, Mona seemed to gather herself. Still clinging to her mother's hand with a tenaciousness that revealed her sense of unbalance, she spoke more freely about the events in the mill, even elaborated at times, as Gemma queried her for facts.

Listening to Mona as they walked rapidly, Gemma started to get a more complete picture of the events leading up to the disappearance. The fact that she could not identify anything out of the ordinary did not lesson her sense of dread. There was one thing; actually, there were two that started to stand out more and more. First, was Aarvid's unusual interest in exploring the mill in the first place. Second, was his fascination with a book just before he…vanished.

As they grew closer to the old structure with its two wings pointed skyward like two arms, she could not help but reminisce some of the tales that had floated around the area about the dark history that surrounded this same mill, tales of unexplained disappearances and murder.

She was startled out of her reverie by the flapping of wings, as a large swan making excited wheezing noises flew right over their heads. Was it her imagination, or had the creature looked her right into the eyes? Had there been sadness in those eyes? There was something else that had happened at that very moment; it had been as if a tender caress had touched her mind. It had lasted only a moment and for that moment she had felt tremendous relief.

Gemma realized that they had both turned to watch the swan fly away. Mona still stood, looking after the rapidly-rising and fading form of the large bird, her hand shading her eyes from the low afternoon sun.

"Mom, did you feel something?" Her little girl's voice was slightly tremulous as she turned and looked at her mother expectantly.

Taken aback, Gemma responded with an amazed, "Yeah…I did!…Strange, but nice!"

"Mom…It felt like that, but different just before Aarvid…" She left the sentence unfinished and continued as if totally lost in the memory, "…It touched my mind just like that but it was different, urgent, more like a presence in my mind. This was softer; it felt like a…goodbye. I think."

Once again Gemma was touched by her daughter's sensitivity. It had felt a little like that for her, too. Gently hugging Mona's shoulders and pulling her closer, she turned to resume their journey toward the old structure. They had barely gone more than a dozen steps when they were met by a swarm of roughly twenty dragonflies. Their startlingly sudden appearance and the fact that they seemed to be flying in some sort of purposeful formation, gave Gemma pause.

Looking after the swarm as it vanished in the same direction as the swan, a feeling of foreboding started to take hold of her. Something strange was indeed going on here; the anxiety that followed was almost too much for her to bear. With a desperate effort, she pushed it down; not really convinced, she told herself, *Maybe Mona just fell asleep for a moment and got confused. Aarvid is in there. He is probably just trapped somewhere inside that mill.*

Carefully Mona stepped inside, firmly grasping her mother's hand to make sure she followed close behind. Little had changed since she and Aarvid first entered that semi-dark interior earlier, except that the brooding darkness was punctuated by a much narrower beam of light that no longer touched the floor. In the diffuse half-light, with her mother in tow, Mona retraced her brother's every step, describing in detail everything he did before entering the small backroom. The retracing seemed to be giving her more confidence. To her it felt as if it confirmed her reality. It had happened this way earlier. She had not been living a bad dream.

Gemma could not believe that her son and daughter had entered such a foreboding structure. *What had made them do such a thing?* She let her daughter lead, listening to her reconstruct all that had happened earlier. Fueled by her mind that kept repeating, *Why had Aarvid done this? ...It was just so unlike him!* each step seemed to increase her unease.

It was much brighter inside the little room at this time of the day than it had been earlier. Among the thick layer of dust that covered everything, a jumble of papers, books, small bottles and other unrecognizable objects littered the floor, and the remaining cupboards as well as on the workbench. Standing in the doorway next to her daughter, Gemma could clearly see two pairs of footprints headed for the workbench in the back of the room; the sight of only one single pair of prints returning toward the door in which they were standing made her heart sink.

They were about to enter into the messy quarter, when the approaching hum of a car engine announced the arrival of the constable. Quickly, they headed outside to meet with the officer.

"Constable Maartens at your service, madam. I hear you are missing your child?" Addressing Gemma, the bald, port little man puffed up his chest, trying to look important. His hands were busy in a futile effort to get the wrinkles out of his grey trousers, while his eyes ran a quick inspection of Gemma, and her dirt-streaked daughter wearing a shirt over her bathing suit.

Extending her hand in greeting, Gemma solemnly said, "Yes, I am the missing child's mother."

While his eyes roamed over the tranquil pond and took in the structure of the old mill looming over them, he asked, "And...uh...how long has he actually been missing?"

The lack of urgency and concern hit Gemma hard. *He is just here because his job requires it. He does not care!* She was about to lash out at him, with the hysteria that was overwhelming her at that realization, when Mona piped up.

"My brother has disappeared inside there." Pointing at the door of the mill, she continued, tears welling up anew in her eyes, her voice quavering. "We were in the back room...We were just reading...uh...my brother was reading this book we found, when he just disappeared."

"Hmm..." Looking skeptical at Mona, he pulled a little notepad from his pocket and took down some notes. "You did go swimming today, did you not?" he asked Mona, his raised eyebrows creasing his forehead.

"Yes, but we went inside there!" She spoke emphatically, adding, "Anke and Wim were here, too! But they did not go inside."

After adding to his notes, he addressed Gemma, "Is that correct, madam?"

Her emotions under control, yet with an edge to her voice, Gemma answered, "Constable, I called you over to ascertain yourself of that. I just arrived with my daughter and..." her voice breaking, "I have not seen a trace of my son!"

After having completed his preliminary interview,

Constable Maartens prepared to enter the old structure. Leading the way for Mona and her mother, he instructed Mona, "I want you to go over everything you did while you were inside with your brother. Leave nothing out!"

Repeating everything she had just a little earlier told her mother, Mona followed the constable to the back room.

When they reached the door to the small room, Gemma chimed in, "It's all exactly the way she told me." Sighing, she added, "You can tell from the footprints…"

"Oh, I know all about footprints," he interrupted. Turning to Mona, and pointing at the workbench, he asked, "You and your brother both ended up at that workbench?" When she nodded, he moved into the small room toward the area of the workbench where the prints stopped.

After a brief inspection of the workbench, he pointed at two dark spots on the bench where dust was missing and asked, "These marks left by a wet bathing suit on this workbench, are they your brother's?"

Once more, Mona nodded her confirmation; pointing at the tome where it lay adjacent to the two marks, its surface gleaming among the dust-covered objects, she added, "He was reading that book. He was acting kind of funny, and he was talking strange." Her voice started to break, and the onset of sobs interrupted her as she finished. "Then…he just…disappeared." Once more, she buried her head in her mother's dress and sobbed quietly.

Gemma realized that Mona truly believed that's what happened. It just sounded so…well, unbelievable. Tears filled her eyes and fear threatened to overwhelm her once more. If she were to believe her daughter's incredible story, she had to accept the fact that Aarvid was indeed lost to them. What incredible events could have caused it to have happened? A whisper in her mind asked the question she did not dare confront. *Could some otherworldly powers be at work? Could Aarvid actually have been dabbling in magic?*

"Now, are you sure you did not fall asleep while he was going through the stuff on this desk?" The constable's question to Mona brought Gemma back from her reverie and snapped Mona out of her fit of sniffling.

"I did not!" was her indignant response. Pointing directly at the tome she continued, "I was leaning up against his legs trying to make him stop reading THAT BOOK!"

Both her mother and the constable looked at the workbench, letting their eyes roam over its surface; neither reacted to the black and red leather tome, with its gleaming golden pages sandwiched between the leather.

What's the matter with them? Can't they see it? It's right there! To make it obvious which item she was talking about, Mona pushed between the two adults, reached out both her hands, and picked up the tome.

Her first surprise was how easy it was to lift. She was about to press the nearly weightless book to her chest when her finger caught something on the binding.

Her second surprise was the object that came out of the binder; reflecting the light with a reddish glitter, the object fell to the ground. Mona had no trouble locating what looked like a bright copper ring among the detritus on the floor. In no time at all she had it in her hand; before she realized she had done so; it's bright coppery shine now a dull reddish hue, it was located snugly on her ring finger.

Her final surprise was that neither of the two adults seemed to have noticed that she had removed the tome, nor that she was now pressing it against her chest. It was as if the brightly-colored book was invisible to them. "I will take care of this," she whispered to herself. "Aarvid would want me to, I am sure." Crossing both arms across the tome, she hugged it closely.

Gemma, her face pale and drawn, was scanning the room without seeing it. To her, nothing that made any kind of sense could possibly explain her son's disappearance.

Constable Maartens was checking the window and the narrow opening that allowed the sunlight to enter the small room. Next, he moved to check the outer wall, looking for any breach large enough to allow a small body to pass through.

"Constable, have you heard the stories about the curse that is supposedly on this mill?" Surprised by Gemma's question, the constable chuckled dismissively before answering, "Well, there are always stories associated with old places like this. I would not pay too much attention to those stories. Your boy will turn up somehow, you'll see. I am sure there is a logical explanation for it all." Giving the room one final scrutinizing stare, he started toward the door. When he reached it, he turned toward Gemma, saying, "I do not see anything else we can do out here. As far as I can tell, your boy is no longer inside this structure." Turning to look at Mona, he added, "I am going to interview your two friends. Maybe they noticed something unusual." After a moment's hesitation he turned to Gemma and added, "I will stop by your house later to pick up a recent photograph of your son."

It was almost dark as they reached home. Gemma, looking defeated, immediately sat herself down at the kitchen table and buried her face in her hands.

Mona seated herself next to her mother and placed the large leather-bound book on the table in front of Gemma. "Look, Mom, I brought the old book. I think it is a magic book. I don't know why, but somehow I think Aarvid is inside of it." While she spoke, she tried without success to pull her mother's hand away from her face.

In the darkness that now enveloped them, Mona was not sure her mother even heard her. Lost in her grief, Gemma reached out to her daughter and pulled her into her. Sobs shook her body as she moaned, "First my dear Aaron, and now my sweet boy. Why? What have I done to deserve this?"

As if in response to her questions, the telephone rang.

The sun was settling on the western horizon when David, wrapped in his black cloak, and his lumbering partner, wearing a scarlet mantle, arrived in the backroom of the old mill. It was immediately clear to David that the tome was no longer there; he could sense its presence slowly moving away.

Mephistopheles was beside himself. "How could this have happened? It had been safe right here for over a century. I feel like Job abandoned by his Lord and left to fend for himself."

David responded calmly, "Your Excellency, I do not think that things are quite that desperate for us. Nothing has changed for you or for me, other than that events have begun that we did not anticipate nor initiate. I am not quite sure what it is that is happening." After sighing deeply, he finished speaking solemnly, "Maybe the prophecy I recited to you is being fulfilled."

"Bah...Prophecy?...Blasphemy!...The ramblings of some uneducated savage!" With clenched fists the scarlet-clad figure stomped his booted feet in angry frustration. Then, raising his pointed finger skyward, he continued, "God himself gave us the responsibility for it when we found the book in the consecrated library of the Abbey of Palermo. That is why it has remained in our charge for more than 700 years." Full of righteous indignation and anger, he towered over David in the semi-darkness of the backroom.

Bending to come eye to eye with the David, he growled, "I will make certain it will return to our charge, I swear to God!"

Looking unblinking into the red reptilian eyes of the Cardinal, the Black Mage shrugged in response to the outburst. After giving his partner a moment to settle himself, he cautioned the still bristling Cardinal, "I do not know if either you or I have the power to change things back to the way they were. Do what you feel you must, Guiseppi, but you'll be on your own. I'll be following after the boy."

Surprised by hearing the use of his birth name, Mephistopheles momentarily forgot his displeasure with the loss of the magic tome. He quickly realized what it meant; there was to be a parting of the way.

"So be it," he grumbled. Then, returning to his own more abrasive person, he made the sign of the cross while sourly mumbling, "Go in peace, my son. May the Lord favor your journey with his blessings." His emphasis on the word "son" meant to convey his displeasure with the use of a name he had long ago discarded, a name that had centuries ago belonged to a sensitive, somewhat fearful young man who had been in awe of David, the Black Mage. He had long ago ceased to be that man.

Thus it was that David, the Black Mage, used his magic to summon transport to attempt catching up with young Aarvid, while Cardinal Mephistopheles went his separate way, prepared to do whatever it would take to regain the magic tome.

CHAPTER 6
FROM FLIGHT TO
FULL FLIGHT

It was all Aarvid could do to keep up with the agile woman, leaping over, and running around obstacles that were scattered in abundance wherever he looked. Painfully, he discovered that the deep layer of dust hid some smaller, sharp edged pieces. Anxious to avoid these pitfalls and eager to keep his bare feet from harm, he focused his attention on the area in front of him. Almost immediately, he could see hazy outlines of debris through the thick layer of dust. It definitely helped in making his scamper toward the narrow crack in the wall less painful.

The sprint toward the opening in the wall offered Aarvid a few moments of relative calm. It gave him time to reflect on how badly he needed the company of his guide and newfound friend. With everything so completely out of proportion, he felt disoriented and completely lost in this strange world. It was as if he was experiencing a real bad dream, except with each adventure he had come to realize that it was all too real and that he had better be prepared for anything.

With Jenn leading the way, they ran into the narrow fissure. Its irregular walls featured jagged edges that protruded inward from both sides. Inside the dark passage Aarvid could hear her light footsteps slowing in front of him. Far behind, out in the backroom, he could hear loud shouting, interrupted by a not so occasional profanity, of their pursuers.

He focused his attention ahead. Almost casually, he achieved a now expected lessening of the darkness. With his senses thus focused he could see Jenn feeling her way along one wall, as well as the sharp turn that was ahead of them.

Just as he caught up to Jenn, he became aware of something unusual intruding on his sharpened awareness. To him, it felt as if he could actually hear someone's thoughts. Someone on the other side of the wall, ahead of them was thinking, *What is going on behind this wall? Why is there so much hollering? Isn't Kirchner out there taking care of things?* Was he imagining it? Instinctively, he reached out and touched Jenn's arm.

She stopped instantly, apparently understanding the cause for his touch and sensing his disquiet. For a moment she went very quiet, then nodded and inclined her head until her forehead touched his, and whispered, "Shh!…Don't think so loud or they'll hear you just like you can hear their thinking. Fortunately, they are a little distracted by the noises of our pursuers and not nearly as sensitive as you are. Try to blank your mind…We'll try to surprise them. We have no other choice." Leaving Aarvid to mull over what she had just told him, she proceeded feeling her way cautiously around the corner, toward the light and the end of the fissure.

Sprinting into the light, her weapon drawn, Jenn disappeared almost instantly behind a large rock. Almost immediately, loud cursing and the sound of weapons clashing told him that she was engaging another group of enemies.

Aarvid felt leaden, his stomach rebellious, and his intestines cramped. He was thoroughly sick of fighting. However, if he failed to join up with Jenn, something might happen to her. He could not tolerate the thought of being alone. Besides, had she not risked her own life for him?

He felt slightly faint; his right hand, slippery with sweat, was holding his sword. Without thinking about it, he had been carrying the blade all along; its blue gleam reminded him of how well he had done with it before. Remembering, he drew a deep breath. Soundlessly, like a shadow, he slunk from rock to rock, determined to help Jenn before it was too late.

In a low crouch, fully focused, holding his weapon in front of him, Aarvid slipped out from the shadow behind a large boulder and came face to face with a battle. It involved Jenn and a handful of monstrous warriors. No one seemed to take notice of him; ignoring the presence of the slight, grimy youngster, their attention was fully focused on Jenn.

Two of the larger creatures, their bodies caked in dark blood, were leaning heavily against some nearby rocks apparently too hurt to rejoin the fray. The remaining three, scrawnier and quicker, were attacking the whirling and slashing young woman with spear-like weapons.

When she slowed for a moment, Aarvid noticed blood on her shoulder. He realized that injured as she was, gasping for air, there was little she could do against her opponents other than stall for a little more time. In addition, muffled shouts and curses could be heard coming from inside the wall.

Overcoming his hesitancy, he surveyed his surroundings trying to find something that would give him some advantage. Moments later, Aarvid was sailing through the air while hanging on to a strand of an old spider web. While he was closing in on the action, he focused on his next move. Once again, it seemed to him as if time slowed down.

Before Jenn's attackers realized what had hit them, Aarvid had dispatched the largest of the group with a vicious kick to the head, sending him crashing to the ground. Letting go of the strand, he landed squarely on the shoulders of another. Remembering his earlier encounters, he squeezed his thighs together to cut off the flow of blood to the head of the warrior he straddled, at the same time slashing his razor sharp weapon downward at another.

Just before the gasping warrior he was mounted on collapsed to the floor, Aarvid leapt away and landed feet first on the ground. Crouched low and sword raised, he turned toward the one remaining warrior. He had just enough time to scramble out of the way as that warrior tumbled into the dust. Blood flowing from a deep cut in the unconscious warrior's shoulder made him nauseous and light headed. His stomach aflutter, he stumbled backward into the arms of Jenn.

They stood there for a few moments. While waiting for his stomach to settle, Aarvid leaned into her with his back and enjoyed the comfort and safety of her one-armed embrace.

Jenn, her face buried in his unruly mop of light brown hair, was gasping for breath. She was exhausted from the exertion and her left shoulder felt like it was on fire. When she regained her breath, she murmured in his ear, "Thank you, Aarvid. I think we scared the others off for now."

After a few more gulping breaths, reluctant to let go of the comfort gained by the feel of his slim frame, she straightened and with her uninjured arm turned him gently around to face her. It took her a couple of seconds to take in the soft brown eyes framed by the child-like features of his face and his young body. Underneath the layer of grime, he was lean with the long muscles of youth. A feeling of awe filled her then. She had hardly believed it the first time, back there up on the workbench, being too occupied herself to take in his accomplishments. There was no denying it this time; exhausted, her shoulder throbbing, she had watched him dispatch of three seasoned veterans in less than a minute. This young man with the heart of a lion was capable of incredible feats that could only be explained by his use of magic, a magic he wielded as if he had been born to it. Yet, he had no idea.

She cupped his dirt-streaked chin with her hand and spoke, her voice tender and filled with awe, "You sure are a pleasant surprise. I never thought you'd be..." She trailed off before finishing, giving him a quick smile, "We'd better get ourselves moving again. It sounds like our pursuers are coming through the wall right now."

Aarvid did not hear the last sentence. Enthralled by the beauty of her face and the depth of her sky-blue eyes, he managed to ask, "Are you hurt badly?"

She ruffled his hair while answering, "Thanks to you I am all right. It's just a scratch."

She added an urgent, "We need to go!"

They moved rapidly through the debris strewn area toward the middle of the room and the part of the mill once used to grind the flour. Behind them, exclamations of dismay indicated that their followers had found the wounded and would temporarily be slowed in their pursuit.

Hurriedly she pointed at the large, broken support beam that slanted upward toward the upper part of the mill. "How fast can you make it up—"

She was interrupted by the appearance of a wiry, bedraggled looking, and bearded hunchback from behind one of the large rocks that was scattered around the bottom part of the beam. He appeared skittish, flinching at every loud noise. It was very obvious that he was nervous to be in a place that could at any time erupt into a battle scene.

"Father, here you are!" Jenn seemed glad to see the old man. "I have been wondering where you were and how long you would wait before coming to help us."

They were approaching a large pile of broken rock fragments when she turned toward Aarvid and pointed at it, saying, "We have to climb to the top of that pile in order to get onto that beam." Next, speaking a little louder over her shoulder, "Father, we have got to make haste and get up on that beam. I believe it is the only way out of this place that may not be blocked off."

They had just begun the climb when Aarvid noticed the shredded remains of a heavy type of cloth. While stooping to retrieve it from a small space between large boulders, he observed that Jenn had stopped a little below him and was addressing her father, who stood looking sullen near the bottom of the pile.

"I am sorry, Dad, but you know this young—"

"I know who he is," he interrupted her brusquely. He stole a quick nervous glance back toward the noise of their pursuers. Then, taking the time to brush matted, long strands of unkempt hair that circled his bald pate from his face and forehead, he looked up at the unimpressive, dirt-streaked Aarvid and hissed angrily, "How could you have involved him? Just look at him! A child!" He stood there a moment shaking his head in disgust. "You have sealed our fate!"

Sounding more desperate, he continued, "Now we are

trapped forever in this miserable world, to become like monsters, products of our own despair." He almost sobbed as he spoke those last words. Nervously, he stole another quick glance in the direction of their pursuers and spat out, "I hope you are happy! See if you can get yourself and him out of this!"

With an agility belying his age, he sprinted off toward a hiding place under the broad, angling beam. Just before he disappeared into the cover of shadowed darkness, he shouted, "Remember what happened to his father!"

As he listened to the exchange, Aarvid had managed to extract what turned out to be a long piece of cloth with shredded pieces dangling from it. While Jenn's father uttered his discourse of displeasure, he was busy wrapping his sword inside the cloth using the shredded pieces to tie it all together. When the bedraggled hunchback took off toward his hiding place, Aarvid was just then busy trying to attach the long bundle to two belt loops of his shorts; he was brought up short by hearing the unsettling and shouted, "Remember what happened to his father!"

Aarvid looked thoroughly bothered when Jenn turned around to face him. She placed a comforting hand on his shoulder and spoke, a sad smile playing across her face, "My father, Burgher Jan, has a way of saying the wrong things. Don't worry about what he said too much. I'll explain…but…" she looked back and down at the approaching noise of their pursuers, "it will have to wait."

Quickly, she inspected and adjusted his rigged up scabbard. Then, making sure to make direct eye contact she implored, "Aarvid, please trust me. Are you with me?"

When he nodded silently, she added, "They are coming closer."

Pointing upward toward the top of the mountain of rubble

and the steeply inclined beam, "Now, let us see how fast you can make it up there." Instantly she was on the move, climbing and clawing her way up.

Before following her, Aarvid stole a quick glance back over his shoulder. He could see a rapidly increasing number of oddly armored warriors bearing down on their location. Determined that this time they would not catch up to engage him and his partner, he scrambled up the steep rough surfaces of stacked boulders toward the slanted beam and the upper reaches of the old mill.

They climbed continuously until they reached the old rusted gears at the top of the milling shaft. They stopped there, both badly in need of a break.

Aarvid looked around. He was way up near the top of the old structure. Old nests were tucked in nooks and crannies everywhere. Some of them had disintegrated and littered the lower beams, along with bird droppings that were liberally sprinkled everywhere. To one side a huge rounded shaft led horizontally from the gears toward an opening at the base of the rounded roof. It was there that a small section of the roof had fallen away, allowing a beam of bright sunlight to enter.

When he turned to ask Jenn her plan, he realized that she was looking down into the dark interior and listening intently.

"I do not see anybody following. It doesn't sound like anyone is following." Watching her nod her head in agreement, he asked, "Do you think they have given up?"

This time, shaking her head and wearing a slight frown, she responded, "No, they will be up here as soon as they agree on who will lead them. I am sure they are not too anxious to do all this climbing; after all, they are all quite bulky."

After a pause, she added, "They could decide to have those horrible bees fly them up here."

"Yellow jackets," he corrected her. "They are nasty yellow jackets."

"Oh, OK. Either way we need to find a way out of here." Having said that, she lifted herself onto the horizontal shaft; moving carefully on its slippery and rounded surface, she headed for the opening in the roof.

She had taken only a few steps when she decided it would be better to proceed together. The way was littered with huge pieces of nesting, giant wood fibers, and other debris, all of it plastered with huge piles of slimy bird droppings. To wander too far from the center of the rounded beam could spell disaster for either one of them; its slippery down-curving surface would send them tumbling down into the darkened interior. Hanging on to each other, they straddled the top of the beam as well as they could while navigating their way over obstacles and through slimy, smelly piles.

Finally they reached the opening in the roof. While they stood still hand in hand on the end of the shaft, they took in the bright scene of that late summer day.

To Aarvid it seemed like it had been days, even though it had only been just a few hours, since he had smelled fresh air and looked at blue sky spotting a few fluffy clouds.

The scene brought on a sudden feeling of loneliness. Gloomy, acutely feeling the loss of companionship from his friends and his sister, Aarvid found a corner on the broad reinforced and curving roof support beam to sit down and gather himself. From his perch he looked down on the now deserted pond. He imagined himself down there splashing around in the cool water with Anke, while Mona and Wim argued about whether skinny Wim had sprouted a chest hair.

Then, excited, he saw something familiar enter the scene below him. Stately, leisurely the large white swan swam to the middle of the pond. Excited, he stood and leaned forward. Would the large bird recognize him? He was just about to shout out to it, when a gust of wind knocked him off his feet. He felt himself lifted off the beam into the air and into the dark interior of the mill. Totally disoriented, he instinctively focused his mind, telling himself, *Find out where I'm heading...Grab hold of something...anything!*

He found himself clinging to a loose piece of roofing that was still connected to the curving roof. Its back and forth movement brought him alternately from a position dangling above the dark cavernous interior of the mill, to one where it just barely passed over the edge of the broad support beam he had been sitting on.

He had just started climbing down, careful to maintain his grip on the many loose fibers of the slowly swinging roof piece, when he heard the cry for help. "Aarvid! Help! I'm slipping!"

Slowly, careful not to lose his grip, he turned toward the sound of her voice. At first he could see no trace of Jenn. Then, as the piece he was clinging to swung over a little, he saw her hand; white from the strain, it clung to a piece of rusty metal that had partially separated from a large nut located on the down slope on the far side of the big shaft.

Aware of the urgency, he focused; once more time slowed. He timed his drop perfect. Floating down slowly, he landed on the edge of the beam feet first while his hands reached for and found soft fibers that protruded from the wood to help steady him.

Aarvid reached her just as her hand was about to lose its hold. Firmly grasping her wrist, he felt himself starting to slide down the curved surface as well. To gain any sort of anchor, he tried folding his body around a section of a large, rusty nut. The rough, sharp edges of the flakey rust bit into his skin. No matter how he tried, he could not stretch his body far enough around the large metal structure to gain perch that way. So, he used the painful bite of the rough rusty edges on his body, as well as what he could cling to with his free hand and feet. He dug himself in, straining to hang on to her without joining her in her down-slide himself. He willed himself to ignore the pain, telling himself, *I can't let her go! She is my only friend here! I've got to get her up on this beam!*

Jenn had resigned herself. She could hang on no longer. She had tried, using every ounce of energy left in her to get another foot or hand hold. It had been to no avail. That sudden gust had picked her up as well and sent her tumbling down the rounded shaft. Where she ended up, the shaft was unusually slippery. She was fortunate to have found any sort of hold at all. When she received no reply after her cry for help, she had correctly assumed that Aarvid had been blown off the ledge as well.

However, when she felt his firm grasp around her wrist, new hope flourished in her. With it came a renewed determination to hang on and to search for any kind of hold with her free hand and feet. Then, surprise! She felt herself slowly lifted upward. Next, a rush of adrenalin coursed through her when one foot found an opening, a foothold. With his help and the foot- and handholds she found, she floundered her way back to the top of the shaft.

Once again, she found herself clinging to him, hugging him fiercely. The temporary comfort and safety gained from the embrace of his slime covered body allowed for a release of the tension that had built up inside of her during her close call with certain death. Grateful, her face buried in his lush brown mop she lost control of her emotions. With her tears running freely, she found herself kissing him.

In a matter of moments she had gathered herself. She told herself, *There is no time for this. Get a hold of your feelings. We are still far from safe.* Gently she pulled his head back and saw the tears wetting his eyes, as well as the wet, smudged trails running down his cheeks. He also had realized how close they both had come to disaster.

She was about to pull him in close to hug him once more, when she noticed the blood on his chest.

"Aarvid, you are hurt!" she exclaimed. Pushing him back to get a better view she noticed the bloody scratches on his stomach and thighs as well. For a moment she was speechless. It just had not occurred to her that he could actually get hurt. Knowing that he possessed the ability to wield the magic she had not even considered such a possibility. It also revealed to her how dedicated he had been to safe her, how much pain he had been willing to endure.

He had wiped the tears from his face, adding smudges to smudges, and stood there his head slightly cocked, a slight smile creasing his lips. Then, pointing at the rapidly healing puncture wound on her left shoulder, he said, "Now we're even, Jenn."

Looking more serious and studying the wound, he remarked, "Boy, I swear that looked much worse right after our fight."

"Aarvid, one of the benefits of being in this realm is that small injuries like these heal up real fast. But…" she ruffled his hair in a rough caress, "that does not make them any less painful."

"Now," she continued, "do you have any suggestion as to how we could get down from here?"

She was surprised by his answer. "Yes, I just found out that if I focus real hard things seem to kind of slow down. I can make myself float down slowly, I think."

"What about me, Aarvid? I cannot do magic like that!"

"We'll have to hang on tight to each other," he suggested, wearing a grin.

She was not going to let him know that there was absolutely NO WAY she would even have considered something as preposterous as jumping from the top of this or any mill, if any other person had suggested it. Coming from Aarvid, even if he was wearing that silly grin, it did not seem that bad an idea, especially if she could hang on real tight.

Instead she asked, "What about all that water down there?"

In response, he turned to look at the pond stretching out below them. After studying it for a few seconds, he pointed at the swan swimming leisurely between the reeds and said, "That swan will help us."

Jenn was about to raise an objection, when grunting sounds coming from the direction of the down-slanted beam could be heard.

"They are coming up the beam," she remarked without emotion. "Very likely, they have some other surprise for us coming from out there." She pointed at the opening in the roof. "Why don't you give that swan a try, Aarvid."

He understood what she meant for him to do, and set out to do it immediately. He moved as close to the edge of the open roof as he dared without risking being blown away again. Sitting down, closing his eyes to help him focus, he reached out with his mind. Reaching out randomly he was almost overwhelmed by the chatter of thoughts. From inside, fairly close to them, there were thoughts like, *That @#$@# woman and her @#$#@ whelp...* and *I am so tired, I think I'm going to die.* While from the outside, a chorus of calls for dragonflies made him aware of what was being planned there.

He narrowed his focus to the area of the pond the swan was

in and sensed something different, something that tickled his sense of vision. He went with it and was surprised by the clear image of rippling water, interrupted by green stalks of reeds. He knew it was what the swan was studying that very moment, and sensed its impatience with the lack of some type of food it was searching for. Instantly, Aarvid overlaid that view with an image of himself feeding the bird, immediately followed by an image of both Jenn and himself standing in miniature form in the opening of the windmill's roof high above the water.

To his surprise, the swan repeated those images coupled with a mix of emotions of relief and impatience that felt like, *Where have you been? I have been waiting for you to come out.*

It was enough. He had figured out how to communicate with the swan. In no time at all he had conveyed their need to the large bird. It responded by raising itself from the water and flapping its wings excitedly. Slowly, gracefully, it swam closer to the mill, its head tilted slightly, trying to catch a glimpse of the young boy and his companion.

By keeping a physical contact with the youngster, Jenn picked up most of what exchanged between Aarvid and the large white bird. She also could hear the heavy breathing and grunting of their pursuers come closer and closer. Preferring to take her chances with Aarvid's scheme rather than stay and fight, she was anxious to be on the move.

After he broke off his mental contact with the bird, he turned to her and asked, "Are you ready?" Silently, she nodded that she was.

Deliberately, with Aarvid in the lead, they moved toward the end of the shaft, prepared to drop down and cling to any object if another gust of wind were to surprise them. Finally, firmly hanging on to one another as well as the skyward pointing arm of the mill, they stood on the furthest part of the axis outside the mill. Standing there, his hand entwined in hers, with blue sky above and the long drop below, Aarvid remembered how he had dropped small model airplanes out of his bedroom window as part of a science experiment, remembering especially his excitement at seeing them float away on the air currents. Emboldened by the memory, he turned to her and said, "Get ready. When you feel a draft coming from below, we'll jump."

A gentle breeze rising up from the water almost knocked them off their perch before they were ready. Regaining his balance, Aarvid turned slightly toward Jenn. "You ready?"

When she nodded, he focused, visualizing the two of them floating down gently on the rising breeze. When he was satisfied that he felt prepared to deal with the unexpected, he commanded, "Go!"

Hanging on tightly to one another, they jumped, away from the mill and into the upcoming breeze. Behind them they could hear the sound of loud expletives while they floated down, away from their frustrated pursuers.

Aarvid experienced a strange calmness throughout the leap. Everything seemed to be happening in slow motion. He felt like he was in total control, almost as if he could control their rate of free fall and where they were falling toward.

To Jenn, the descent was amazingly smooth. Still, afraid to let go of Aarvid, she hung on as the wind carried them to the outstretched canvas of the down-pointing arm of the windmill.

When they landed into the worn, down-sloping canvas, it was as if they were sliding down a soft flexible chute. After shooting out of the bottom end of the canvas covered wing, they experienced a few more moments of free fall before landing softly into fluffy white feathers, onto the back of the suddenly enormous swan.

To Aarvid, it had felt like he was pulling all the strings, their soft landing onto the back of the swan just as he had planned. However, his satisfaction with his accomplishment was quickly overshadowed by the memory of seeing that flock of dragonflies passing by, each carrying an armored warrior. They had been headed up toward the opening in the roof of the old mill. It would not be long before they would figure out that their targets had acquired the assistance of the large, powerful swan.

Aarvid shared with Jenn what he had observed during their descent. She had her eyes squeezed shut for most of the way down, consequently had not seen the flock of dragonflies and their mounted riders. She agreed with his decision to get away from the mill immediately. Focusing, he conveyed the image of the mounted dragonflies to the swan along with emotions of fear and feeling upset. It was immediately returned back to him, followed by images of the large bird taking off from the pond and flying away, up into the blue sky.

With its beak emitting a loud rumbling squawk, the large swan extended its head and flapped its wings with short, powerful strokes. Now, appearing as big as a large jet to its two passengers, it rapidly gained speed and lifted itself away from the surface of the pond, its wings beating slower and with even greater power.

They had just reached a height just above that of the treetops when Aarvid, peeking over the thick layer of feathers, saw his mother and sister on the road, walking hand in hand toward the windmill. Quickly, his mind projected their image to the swan, conveying with it a sense of loss and love.

The large bird responded instantly, dipping one of its huge wings so that it would pass close by Gemma and Mona.

Aarvid watched as they approached rapidly. He saw the drawn, frantic look on his mother's face, as well as the intensity with which Mona was conversing with her. He also saw and felt their reaction to his telepathic, *I love you! I love you! Goodbye!*

Through tears, sobbing uncontrollably, he watched them shrink into the distance as the swan quickly regained altitude and flew onward, away from the old windmill, leaving their pursuers far behind.

CHAPTER 7
HAPHAZARD
HAZARDS

They had flown above the few fluffy white clouds that intermittently passed below them for some time when Jenn decided it was time to help Aarvid come out of his grief induced despair.

Jenn had felt his anguish at having to leave his mother and sister with no assurance that he would see them again in the near future. Memories of her own banishment at the age of thirteen, a long time ago, still stirred strong emotions that washed over her as she watched him suffer. Curled up, his body racked by intermittent sobs, he had looked every bit the eleven-year-old who was being torn from those he loved. Seeing and feeling him suffer so, she had also felt a terrible guilt. She could not help but feel that it was at least in part her fault that he was in this predicament.

While the swan rocked them with its powerful rhythmic strokes, she touched him gently on the shoulder. Her voice slightly hoarse, she asked, "Aarvid, is there anything I can do?" When he did not respond, she waited a moment before asking him, "Is there anything you want me to explain?"

He picked up his head from where it had been buried between his knees and looked at her glancing sideward, hesitant to reveal his tear-stained face.

Jenn could not help herself. In spite of the situation, she could barely stifle her laughing at the picture presented by his smudged features. The combined effect of the cleansing from tears with rubbed-on dirt from hands and knees, produced a most comical effect; his skin free of dirt around his still wet eyes and mouth, with dark, nearly black stains on his cheeks, chin, and forehead, he looked absurdly the sad clown. Sliding between the feathers that separated them, she moved closer, reached her arm around his far shoulder, and pulled his dirt-streaked face into her. After a moment, she was rewarded by his responding hug. They sat there hugging one another silently, until she asked, "Well...did you have a question for me?"

Aarvid appeared to gather himself. Still seated, his body straightened as he looked her in the eyes, a frown creasing his forehead. "Where are we anyways?"

She understood what he meant and answered, "We're in the magic realm, Aarvid. As you may have noticed..."

Jenn took time to explain about the magic realm, why it was nearly impossible for those inhabiting it to return to the normal world, and why they were being followed. She left out any reference to his father, instead referred to his ability to use magic as the reason they were being hunted while at the same time crediting his effective use of it for their successful escape.

Aarvid had busied himself trying to catch a glimpse of the land far below, and trying to converse mentally with the large bird. At first, attempting a mental conversation had been like learning a new method of communicating for both of them; a bit complicated initially, it got easier as the swan caught on quickly.

"Ghooinch…Ghooinch," was the direct reply released into the turbulent air at Aarvid's insistent attempts at finding out if it had a name.

Gons? responded Aarvid mentally. *Is it Gons?* Unable to speak into the howling wind, he had persisted in communicating telepathically, using images associated with feelings and words.

He was surprised by the swan's response, "Ghoinch," accompanied by images of a young duckling's futile efforts at staying afloat and even more useless efforts at fluttering flight. Aarvid got the strong impression the large bird was trying to make fun of him, especially since the young duckling wore his face. It was followed by a resigned, "Ghoinch."

Responding to Jenn's chuckling laughter, "What? What is so funny?"

"You mean you did not get that?" she asked, laughing.

"I think Gons was trying to poke fun at me," he answered, a bit uncertain.

"I am as surprised as you must be to realize that our large feathered friend has such a good sense of humor." Bemused, she continued, "I think it said, 'Your hearing is about as good as your swimming and flying.'"

She went on in a more serious tone, "I am amazed at your ability to communicate telepathically in such a complex manner, using images coupled with feelings. It took me years to get mental exchanges between myself and normal people down. I am still not really as good as you are in communicating with intelligent animals like Gons here."

"Well, uh, it's a little bit like watching television, except it is in your head and, instead of sound, you kind of feel or sense what it is trying to tell you." Trying to explain to Jenn why it worked for him, he went on, "It just takes a little getting used to. I always wanted to talk to the swan when I fed it bits of my lunches. It was always there watching us when we went swimming and…"

He was interrupted by mental images and impressions coming from the swan that conveyed something like, *I really do not understand why you wanted to plant your face on that other featherless creature that so often was there with you. She was even noisier in the water than you were.*

Under the layer of grime, Aarvid's face had gone very red. Embarrassed, fumbling for a response, he sputtered, *You knew? You could see my thoughts?*

The only response he got was a brief flash of two featherless ducklings, one wearing his face, the other Anke's, with their bills entwined, along with an emotion akin to a chuckle.

Jenn, who had noticed Aarvid's embarrassment decided to change the subject and asked, "Aarvid, could you ask our feathered eavesdropper if he can find us a quiet little place where we can clean up some before it gets too late in the day?"

The large bird banked sharply, zeroing in on a smooth stretch of water that was surrounded by a narrow border of rushes. While it spiraled down in rapid descent, Aarvid could see other smaller and larger splashes of water. It indicated the presence of swamps and small ponds beyond the rapidly expanding body of deep blue water that was their target. In no time at all they were flying just above the water of a small lake.

After a flutter of extended wings, followed by a gentle splash, they were floating gracefully on its sky blue surface. With late afternoon rays sparkling golden from its gently rippling surface, they headed for the nearest patch of dry sandy shore.

It was part of a small island in the middle of the shallow body of water. Its highest point consisted of a nest built of packed mud and dried rushes. Feathers liberally littered its dark brown mottled surface, indicating that at one time it must have been used by waterfowl. Moss was growing around its edges and in places sprigs of light green grass sprouted through the tufts of feathery down. A couple of buttercups crowned the small rise. Their golden flowers extended into the air like large inverted parasols.

From the smooth sandy shore, Aarvid surveyed the peaceful and scenic surroundings while Jenn stretched the stiffness out of her joints. It amazed him how different everything looked, especially from close up. The nest, its walls of sun baked mud reinforced by huge brown blades of rushes, looked like a towering fortress. The large feathers protruding from its walls and top looked strangely out of place.

He could not help thinking of how much fun it would be to have Anke, Wim, and Mona here to swim and picnic. Thinking of his friends and sister brought a pang of anguish.

Before he could get too caught up in yearning for his friends and sister, Jenn brought him back to their present circumstance by saying, "Aarvid, I probably smell and look as disgusting as you, so I really must scrub myself down and clean up." Laughing at the look of disgust on his face as he checked his lower body and shorts, she added, "Yes, you are disgustingly smelly and dirty. Try scrubbing down with mud. It works great. Also, don't go around that point over there for a little while, will you?"

She had gone no more than a few steps, when she turned and reminded him, sounding more serious, "Aarvid, don't let down your guard. Things that you never considered a hazard before can now be terribly dangerous. Small creatures like little minnows that can swallow you whole, bugs that can capture you and cut you in half, and many other things. Try not to use magic if you can help it. Let out a good yell if there is trouble." To make certain he understood, she asked, "All right? You will be careful?" She waited for his response before turning away.

Aarvid nodded silently and flashed a broad, reassuring smile. When Jenn turned, he turned, untied his sword, and with a running start dove into the cool cleansing water.

The pain around his ankle was excruciating. It was so intense he could not think of anything else. Next, Aarvid's mind was drowning in fear that his ankle was being ripped off. Totally overwhelmed by pain he let out a moaning, "Augh, my leg!" Thoughts flashed through his mind. *I will lose my foot at the ankle, unless I do something!... Right, I can do magic!... Ice! I need ice!* Determined, he focused on the image of ice forming around his trapped ankle.

Already the pain seemed to be less. Careful not to move too sudden and risk another wave of pain, he looked down. His ankle was caught in a vise of two huge pincers. He recognized the creature then; a huge dragonfly larva, its six legs moving slowly, was dragging him into deeper water. Aarvid had also noticed the shimmer of white ice forming around his ankle. The pain was almost bearable but he still felt robbed of the strength needed to resist the powerful force that tugged on his leg.

He had to get free before the creature could drown him. Water was sloshing up to his chin. Panicked, he yelled, "Jenn, I am being pulled into deep water! Something's got my leg! Help me!"

With every ounce of strength he could muster, he yanked his leg free. His arms and legs churning the water to foam, fearful of getting caught again, he swam back to shore. He could not shake the realization that he had just experienced his closest call since the start of this adventure. When his hands touched loose debris that littered the bottom of the shallows he stood up. Bent over, leaning on his knees, he tried to catch his breath. Intensely relieved, he gingerly tested his still ice encased and throbbing ankle.

When he realized that everything was still attached and working, anger replaced fear. He was angry with himself for being so careless and not heeding Jenn's warning. Instead, he lashed out with his anger at the dragonfly larvae, creating in his mind an image of the bug protruding from the jaws of a fish as it chopped on it.

He was still wiping water out of his eyes when he heard churning of water behind him. When he turned to look, it was just in time to see a large minnow, its head clear of the foaming water. It was out of the water just for a moment, but in that moment Aarvid had noticed the larvae's head and pincers still sticking out from its jaws.

In the next instant, two arms wrapped themselves around his chest, lifted him up and carried him out of the hip deep water. Aarvid knew it was Jenn, her cool, wet skin and the soft pressure of her bosoms against his back comforted and relaxed him.

When they were out of the water completely, she released him with a short, "Wait!" Then, turning him by the shoulder to face her, she lit into him, her face flushed with anger. "Aarvid, don't you ever scare me like that again! That fish could have…" Now shaking her finger, not looking quite as agitated, "Don't you ever!" Then, as tears welled up in her eyes, "Aarvid, are you all right?"

Aarvid was slightly bewildered by the sight of her standing there, naked except for a large leaf-like object that only partially covered her. He had temporarily forgotten the pain in his still throbbing ankle. Struggling between fascination with, and admiration of her physical gifts, he felt his face flush and lowered his eyes. He heard her emotion filled question, asking if he was all right, just before he was pulled into her bosom in a tight hug; smothered by the objects of his fascination, he could only nod.

He was brusquely pushed back at arms length and heard her ask, her head slightly cocked, "You are sure?" She seemed herself again, regal and confident, not at all embarrassed by her lack of cover. In a tone that was almost scolding, she continued, "Now, will you be more careful?"

Jenn waited for his demure nod before continuing in the same tone, "I do not know how long it will take for our pursuers to find us. You made it a lot easier for them by your powerful burst of magic just now." Not waiting for his response, she went on, "Well, I am going to finish what I started." With that, she turned and walked off. As if she could feel his following stare, she waved her greens without turning and ambled on.

Aarvid felt suddenly exhausted. Slowly, he sat down on the damp ground. His head supported on crossed arms that were wrapped around folded knees, he stared at the now calm looking water. Ashamed at having placed Jenn and himself in a position where their pursuers could identify their location, he reviewed what had happened.

He concluded there had really been no other choice but to use magic to free himself from the powerful insect; remembering the size and power of it, he shuddered. He was not quite certain that the thing with the fish eating the bug had been his doing. Sure, he had wanted it to happen, but, did that mean that he had caused it to happen? A little voice in his head kept repeating, *Sure you did! Remember, you have the power of magic.* He remembered his anger and how badly he had wanted to hurt the creature. Maybe he had caused it to happen after all. It was all very confusing. He promised himself then, *I am going to have to be more careful. I can't just wish for things to happen any more without thinking about it first.*

Aarvid woke with a start. He must have dosed off. An involuntary shiver ran through his chilled body as he straightened his stiff joints. The pain in his ankle had mostly disappeared. Gingerly, he walked into the lengthening shadows to retrieve his sword, thinking, *I've got to find something to cover myself with. It's going to get a lot cooler.* With an effort, he pushed aside thoughts of home, a steaming bath, dry clothes, and a warm dinner. The rumble in his stomach was real; he really was hungry! Thinking out loud, shaking his head, he mumbled, "Somehow, I've got the feeling that is going to be very different as well."

He was staring at the towering walls of the mountainous nest, looking for something that might be edible, when he heard a rustling noise over to his right. He was scanning that part of the nest-wall looking in the direction from where the noise had come, when, in the corner of his eyes, he caught the movement.

They were whiskers and they disappeared behind a small clump of moss. While he tied his weapon to his belt loops, Aarvid backed away and over to his right trying to get a better view. He kept his eyes on the spot on the side of the nest where he had seen the whiskers. Hidden in the shadows of a large hole, he could just barely make out the dark nose and shiny eyes of a mouse.

Compared to its surroundings, it must have been a small

field mouse. From his perspective, it looked more the size of an elephant. When Aarvid probed the mouse mentally, he read puzzlement; it was confused, wondering whether the little creature below should be considered food or danger. Deciding that he did not like being considered as dinner, he immediately placed an image in the rodent's mind of a large shadow in the shape of a small hawk moving over their location. With a jump and a small, "Squeak," it turned and disappeared into the hole.

"Hmm, that's almost too easy," he chuckled, thinking out loud. "Maybe it's got some food stashed in there." Not knowing of a better place to look, he proceeded to climb the steep side of the nest toward the cave-like entrance.

Aarvid felt dwarfed by the size of the entrance to the mouse's hideout. He was not sure if it was wise to enter the cavernous tunnel; its walls were packed down smooth, showing white roots and trickles of moisture. *I'll go only as far as I can see,* he promised himself, hoping he would not have a run-in with the monster mouse. The rumbling in his stomach and the possibility of finding something edible motivated him to give it a try. Slowly, sword in hand, he ventured into the dark tunnel.

Every time he was about to decide to turn around because it was too dark to see, his eyes somehow adjusted to the dimness and he could see clearly once again. After several turns and what seemed like a long time of stealthy advance, he heard a rustling noise around the next bend of the dark tunnel.

Projecting the image of a large hungry snake, looking for a tasty mouse, he crept around the bend. Totally focused on projecting the image of a hungry snake onto the unsuspecting mouse, he did not pay attention to where he placed his feet. Just as he came face to face with the elephant-sized creature, he tripped and found himself lunging forward. For just a split second the mouse was frozen in place, then, displaying amazing agility, it did a reverse somersault and scurried off into a side tunnel, making disgruntled little squeaks.

The nest was amazingly neat. Composed of downy tuft, grass and pieces of cloth, it looked very comfortable. Off to one side, Aarvid could make out a tunnel; the distinct smell of rodent waste came from that direction. On the opposite site of the nest, he could see the outline of another chamber. When he entered it, he discovered that it was filled with a supply of nuts and seeds. He had found the food supply he was looking for.

Returning to the nest, he poked it with his sword to free some of the pieces of cloth. He was about to pull a piece free, when a small dark critter bopped its head out from between the nesting materials. It turned its faceted eyes toward Aarvid, leaped cleanly over his head, and disappeared in the same direction as the mouse. When Aarvid poked the nest in other places, another three dark insects leaped out of the heap of bedding and bounced off in the same direction. Amused, Aarvid snickered. "I'll be darned, that mouse has fleas for pets."

After freeing some good-sized, fairly clean pieces of cloth from the nest, he wrapped his booty of nuts and seeds in them, and slid them onto his sword. With his load hanging from his shoulder, he headed back. He felt upbeat, proud of himself. On his own, he had managed to acquire something to eat for himself and Jenn.

In no time at all, he was at the mouth of the tunnel. Fresh air filled his lungs as he proudly stepped out of the mouth of the tunnel, into the shadowed world of the waning day. After having climbed down onto the sandy plain of the narrow beach, he swung his load from his shoulder and bent over to inspect his plunder. A painful pinch of his buttocks brought him up short. Instantly, he straightened and turned, bringing his sword up defensively.

The small sand crab was partially suspended, hanging from fibers projecting from the cliff-like nest with most of its legs while a couple rested on the sand. It's stalked, compound eyes stared Aarvid squarely in the eyes. To Aarvid it looked more like a tank that got squashed.

When a thick pincer tried to probe him, he slashed at it with his sword. His weapon bounced harmlessly off the thick chitin. With amazing quickness, the other clawed pincer grabbed a hold of the sword and nearly wrenched it free of his hands. Determined not to let go of his only weapon, he grabbed it with both hands. In the next instant, Aarvid felt himself lifted off the ground and carried up along the near vertical surface of the towering nest. With the ground rapidly receding below him, he was totally preoccupied with just hanging on.

Aarvid regained some of his wits when his feet touched the ground again on top of the nest. He knew that he was totally outmatched by his armored adversary and his only recourse was using magic once again. Thinking quickly while hanging on determinedly to his weapon, he remembered the effect of the bird's shadow on the mouse. Unsure whether the little tank-like creature would be intimidated by a shadow, he focused fully on the real thing. He was surprised by the swiftness of the shadow that swooped down and…

The seagull flying over the nest was suddenly alerted to the presence of a little crab, perched right there on top of the empty nest. It swooped down and, without slowing scooped it up with its bill.

Suddenly, Aarvid found himself airborne as well. When the startled crab let go of the sword and the boy attached to it, Aarvid experienced free fall again. Surprised by the rapid succession of events, he instinctively wished for a parachute or one of those big yellow buttercups he had seen growing out of the nest, to float down with. Before he had fully completed the thought, he landed squarely in the middle of one of the yellow buttercups that decorated the top of the empty nest.

There was an explosion of pollen all around him. Little fluffy yellow balls were stuck in his hair, under his arms, between his legs, and to various other places of his body.

"It's a good thing nobody can see me like this. Mona would call me a yellow puffball," he mumbled, pulling the sticky balls off his body.

After removing most of the sticky balls from his body, he pulled the pollen stalks aside and was rewarded with a nice view of his surroundings. To the west, looking into the lowering sun, open water glittered with reflected sunlight. To the north and east, a narrower body of water bordered by rushes with, rising above them, an abundance of blue, white, and golden splashes from wildflowers. It was from that direction that Aarvid at first heard, and then saw, an approaching bumblebee. Drunk with nectar and loaded down with yellow pollen, it headed straight for him.

He had never been very brave around the noisy buzzers when he was regular sized. Now, with the fuzzy creature the size of a small car, he was petrified and ready to leap from the flower and take his chances. With an effort, he restrained himself and noticed that the noisy creature had veered off to visit a neighboring flower instead. Relieved, he squeezed himself between the golden petals and started climbing down the hairy stalk. The long projections provided ample foot- and handholds. Making his way down rapidly, he did not notice the green creature, the size of a large dog, until his foot bumped into it.

The aphid hardly noticed him. Busily sucking the nutrient-rich juice from the stalk, it was much too preoccupied. Aarvid slowly edged himself closer until he was eye to eye with the creature. He studied it closely and noticed that its rotund abdomen seemed to be leaking some clear fluid. Curious, he reached out and touched the liquid, accidentally rubbing the creature's abdomen. He was rewarded with a handful of clear, sticky residue. At first, Aarvid placed a small amount in his mouth; encouraged by its rich, sweet texture he continued rubbing the aphid's abdomen and sampling its sweet secretion until he felt quenched. Before continuing his descent, he looked down and noticed several pollen balls still stuck to the back of his shorts. Reacting to a spontaneous inspiration, he pulled one off, rubbed it in the fluid oozing from the aphid's abdomen, and placed it in his mouth. The flavor was rich and rewarding. Before Aarvid continued down the stalk, he had polished off all the remaining pollen balls that were stuck to him.

Refreshed by his unexpected meal, he quickly made his way down into the nest and, careful not to attract the attention of any more strange critters, found his way down to the shore.

The wrapped bundles of food were right where he had dropped them. Hoping to dry them some more, he spread them out on a piece of dried leaf. Next, he washed the pieces of cloth and hung them up to dry as well. Relaxed, feeling the effects of the day's exertion, and his recent meal, Aarvid stretched himself out on a dry, sunny part of the beach. Almost as soon as his head touched the soft ground, he was asleep.

The first hints of yellow and orange were visible in the fluffy clouds of the eastern sky, when Jenn reappeared from around the bend and approached on the narrow beach. Seeing Aarvid asleep, stretched out on the dry sand, with next to him the drying seeds and nuts that he had collected, she sat down next to him and gently shook him.

He woke with a start, looked around momentarily disoriented, and then, while rubbing the sleep out of his eyes, flashed her a smile.

Before he had a chance to speak the question that was on his face, she said, "I see that you've been busy." Pointing at the food and the strips of cloth, "Where did you get all that?" Once again, forestalling his answer and nodding at the drying pieces of cloth, "If I had known you had those, I could have done an even better job with this."

She pulled a crudely made vest from behind her back. Enjoying the surprised look on his face, she added, "I just thought you might want to wear something in addition to that skimpy pair of shorts."

"Wow, thanks! It's great!" he exclaimed, accepting it. Aarvid studied the garment and was surprised at how light it was. Shivering, he suddenly realized how cold he felt.

While stroking the hair out of his face, she offered, "Why don't you try it on. It's the pullover type."

Without bothering to get up, he pulled the vest over his head and tied the loose fibers at the top to tighten it. Hugging his knees, he felt warmth returning to his cold body. He turned to her, smiling, and said softly, "Thanks. It's perfect. I am feeling warmer already."

While thanking her, he took note of how beautiful she was. Her soft gold-blond hair with its rough-cut, boyish look framed her still youthful face, emphasizing her delicate features. Her now clean, but threadbare clothes barely concealed the curves of her slim, athletic body. He felt like a student admiring a beautiful teacher, wishing he was older.

"Are you going to sit there and grow roots or are we going to find us a safe place to spend the night?" Jenn's question brought him back to their situation. Especially, when she reminded him, "You used some pretty powerful magic earlier this afternoon. Remember? I am certain that they have honed in on us by now."

As if to emphasize Jenn's last statement, Aarvid felt a slight tingle in his mind. Getting up, searching the sky, he could not see anything approaching. Yet, he spoke urgently, "Jenn, we've got to hurry away from here! I feel them coming closer, right now!"

Commander Crawitz and his soldiers had watched as the swan flew off, taking with it their quarry. There was nothing he could do other than direct his platoon to continue on their dragonflies and try to follow the young boy and his companion long enough to get a sense of their direction. It was soon apparent that his choice of transportation had been a poor one. The insects had such a short attention span that their riders were growing tired of constantly having to repeat their instructions. Just keeping them airborne proved difficult.

When Crawitz decided he had no choice but to change mounds, he and his platoon had pretty much lost contact with the swan and its passengers. A flock of four pigeons, returning to their cages, proved to be too good an opportunity to pass up.

The platoon was soon making rapid progress. By mentally overriding the birds homing instinct, Commander Crawitz had them flying in the same direction he had last observed the disappearing swan.

Crawitz was beginning to belief that they had wasted their efforts in trying to catch up with the young boy and his female companion. With his mind scanning desperately, searching for any trace of magic, he experienced a sudden, powerful surge. There was no mistaking its direction. The suddenness and the extent of magic power that had been applied awed him. He kept his mind tuned to where it had come from while directing his pursuit. He was rewarded for his persistence, because at various intervals, he continued to sense someone using magic in a way he had never experienced before. All of it had the same feel; it was coming from the same person. He realized that the source must be the young boy and once more wondered what he was to do if they ever caught up with the pair.

As the sun sunk lower on the western horizon, the doves grew more difficult to control. Their homing instinct was strong and it was with great difficulty that the platoon managed to stay together. The trail of the boy and his companion finally led them to an area dominated by swamps and low-lying pasture land.

With the promise of a colorful sunset painting the eastern sky, they finally homed in on a small tranquil lake. Traces of magic were strongest near a small patch of dry silt, dominated by an old nesting site. There was no one in sight.

Led by Crawitz, the platoon landed on the deserted nest. They were rewarded by fresh evidence that their quarry had been there just moments before. Fresh pollen were scattered everywhere, a torn claw from a small crab still clung to the side of the nest, and tracks were scattered all over the beach below. Excited, the members of the platoon climbed down to investigate. It was then that the pigeons took off, resuming their journey home. Crawitz tried desperately to call them back, but it was of no use.

They had explored the entire little island, even the cave inhabited by the mouse. Relative to the size of the warriors of the platoon, the little rodent was the size of a rhino or small pachyderm. Still spooked by Aarvid's magical snake, it had bolted from its nest when the warriors entered its cave, trampling several of them.

It was getting dark and still Crawitz had not managed to get them new transportation. Two of his warriors were too injured to continue. That left five, including him, to continue the pursuit. With the trail getting cold, the commander was at wit's end. He was about to direct his warriors to settle in for the night, when out of the impending darkness a small barn owl appeared. In a flurry of feathers it settled on the rim of the tall nest wall. Its large yellow eyes looked down at Crawitz and the remainder of his soldiers. After a moment it blinked, closed its eyes, tucked its head under its wing and went to sleep.

The commander and his small band had been momentarily startled by the sudden appearance of the large night predator. They were relieved to discover it had brought the Black Mage, David, and a companion. They were completely taken off guard when they discovered that his companion was none other than their old nemesis Burgher Jan.

David had left his meeting with the Cardinal more upset than he had let on. He had been worried for some time that his long time friend and partner was becoming increasingly more territorial and bloodthirsty as the years went by. Now, his partner appeared intent on retaking the book of magic from a very young girl when, essentially, it should not matter to him. What worried the Black Mage even more was how he would go about getting it back. David just hoped that he was right and that the magic was manipulating events, in which case whatever he did would not change the eventual outcome. Hopefully, she would hold her own. His priority was to follow the young boy, to see for himself where events would take the youngster and his troublesome companion. At least, something inside of him was telling him that he should.

David took great care to obtain all the details of what had transpired during the exchanges between the guards and the youngster, and his equally dangerous companion, by interviewing many of the scores of wounded who had remained behind inside the mill.

Finally, he gathered all those that were alert enough to understand what he intended to tell them. He started by admonishing them. "Guardsmen, I am not ungrateful for your sacrifice. However, all of your suffering you have brought upon yourselves by not following the directives I had given you." When some of the guards started to protest, he raised his hand to silence them, and continued, "If you received other orders, or if your commander changed the orders I gave, I will deal with that personally and at a later date. Just in case any of you are not clear about what I require of you, I will repeat the orders once again. Woe to those who fail to abide by them this time!" He calmly surveyed the men who were gathered, before continuing, "If by chance the young boy and the young lady known by the name of Jennifer, also referred to as Jenn, happen to return here, you are to use any non-violent means to convince them to wait for me. You are to let me know immediately if and when you make contact. Is that understood?"

Next, the Black Mage explained that he was going after the fleeing pair and would return only when they did.

He was interviewing one of the warriors who had been unable to
acquire a mount to join in the pursuit, and who had witnessed

their incredulous escape, when the bent figure of Burgher Jan appeared.

"Excuse me, uh, David," he stumbled, looking torn between flight and continuing. Finally, when David nodded for him to continue, he said, "I heard what you told those men just now." Once again, waiting for David to nod, he continued, sounding more at ease, "You know, I'd just as soon spit in your eye than ask for a favor." He looked down at his feet for a moment before looking David in the eye while saying, "I made a grievous error. I was short with my daughter when I should have been paying closer attention to what she wanted to tell me. Will you allow me to accompany you?"

David could not believe what was happening. Burgher Jan had been a sworn enemy for too many years to count. There he stood, asking for a favor. Things were changing indeed. "If you promise to let bygones be bygones, I will be glad to oblige." Suddenly realizing how this might make it easier for him to approach the fleeing pair, he added, "As a matter of fact, I would consider it an honor."

"So, they have left." David looked tired and seemed annoyed. "Do you have any idea what direction they went?"

Commander Crawitz responded formally, "Yes, Your Honor, they have left. I suspect that they continued in the same general direction. If we had not lost our mounts, we would have been heading in that direction." He made a curt motion with his hand pointing north north-east. "I detected small traces of magic coming from that general heading, sir."

The Black Mage pensively stroked his chin. Then, to Burgher Jan's surprise, he turned to him and asked, "What do you think, Jan? Do you think they would have gone much farther today? I would think they must be exhausted by now."

"I do not know, David," the scrawny, stooped figure replied. To Commander Crawitz's consternation, he continued informally, "You know that daughter of mine? The more you press her, the harder she pushes herself. Of course, I can't say about that boy. My guess is they went as far as they needed to go to be safe."

David nodded acquiescence, turned to Crawitz and ordered, "Commander, please get your able men together and ready to go. We'll be off as soon as we can!"

The steady rhythmic beating of the wings, the rustling of air passing over feathers, and the occasional glow of lights from little towns far below appearing and disappearing, confirmed that they were making progress. Tired, yet refreshed by the food and drink, they had been traveling in darkness for nearly an hour.

"Are you sure of where you are bringing us?" Aarvid asked the big bird telepathically, not having the slightest idea of where they were right now.

"Gweeach," was the honked reply. It was accompanied by images of peaceful marshland and feelings of content.

Aarvid was seriously bothered by a growing feeling of helplessness. It was not a lack of confidence in his feathered friend, nor a lack of comfort that was causing it. He felt as if it was going to overwhelming him. Sure, Jenn told him earlier, right after they left the small lake and were snacking on dried seeds, that he would become the most powerful mage in the magic world. She told him that he needed time to learn how to wield the magic before it was safe to return.

Aarvid really liked Gons and admired Jenn, and would trust his newfound friends with his life if he had to. However, right now he wanted to be home; staying with his two friends would only keep him further from that goal. If only he knew which magic spell to use to make all his troubles go away, to bring him back to normal, to sit on the table and have dinner with his mom and sister, to be able to look forward to sleeping in his own bed. He had not wanted any of this magic stuff.

There were no answers in the constant rumble of air rushing over his head. He felt very much alone, trapped and helpless. Feelings of homesickness and self pity overwhelmed him then. With tears coursing down his cheeks, he could barely stifle the sobs as he tried to hide his unhappiness from his friends.

Both Jenn and the swan were very much aware of his mood. Jenn especially agonized over what she could do to help him accept their situation. She decided that maybe now was a good time for her to share some of her own story with him.

"Aarvid," Jenn's voice intruded out of the darkness, bringing him back from his darkening mood, "there are probably a lot of things that you would rather hear, but they might be lies. I know the pain you are feeling. I have been dealing with the same feelings that you are dealing with for about three hundred years."

She could see his head jerk up at hearing that and she could feel his eyes scrutinize her anew. Before he could interrupt, she went on. "At first, I was truly helpless in this realm. Over time, I learned how to deal with it and I managed to learn a few tricks that helped me survive."

She continued by telling him her story, of how David the Black Mage had put her into the magic realm at the age of thirteen so that he could force her into a relationship, and how she had managed to evade him all these years.

She told him about Cardinal Mephistopheles the other power in the magic realm; far removed from being a pious creature, he loved his power and used his guardsmen freely to persecute the citizens of the magic realm.

"Of all the living beings in the magic realm, Cardinal Mephistopheles is the most dangerous and unpredictable. I've heard that he is like the devil incarnate. He gets his thrills out of placing pain on others. Especially, he loves burning them alive."

"What about all the others?" Aarvid interjected. "They all looked like monsters and I could read their thoughts. They were…eh…like mutants. You are the only one I have met in this world that looks normal, not like the others."

"Hmm…" she chuckled, "I don't know if I should consider that a compliment. Anyway, thanks."

After a deep breath, she continued, sounding very serious, "That's the other part about the magic, Aarvid. In this realm, people can't hide from their true selves nor can they hide it from others. Since others can tune into your thoughts, there is little use in fighting it." She added gravely, "In a very short time you change into the image of your soul."

"What do you mean?" he asked. Before Jenn could address his confusion, he added, "Is that why those warriors were so grossly misshaped, like mutants?"

"In part, yes!" she explained. "It is hard for them to recognize those changes in themselves. In many ways they just become who they perceive themselves to be. In addition, they have added to the effect of those changes by wearing insect claws and armor." After pausing to reflect on what she just explained to him, she added, "You'll recognize what I mean when you look closely at the citizens of this realm when you meet up with them."

"They're not all mutant warriors?" he asked, incredulous.

"Well, you've seen my father. There are many, actually a

very great number of beings that inhabit the realm. Some like my father, and some not."

When she did not elaborate further, he tried to remember the images of the warrior creatures that he had met in battle today. On reflection, they had indeed all been very different from one another.

Her voice interrupted his musings. "As you have already discovered, there are some benefits to being in the realm of magic. Not only can you tune into someone else's thinking, you can even communicate telepathically with animals.

"To me, the worst thing about being in the realm is that it is like carrying a lifelong sentence multiplied a hundred times. In many ways it is like being imprisoned. Once you find yourselves in it, you cannot get out unless you can control the magic like the mages." Jenn spoke those words with a slight edge to them. Aarvid clearly sensed that she was far more frustrated about this than she was letting on. He had not tried to tune into her unspoken feelings; to him that just was not right. He did not need to read her mind to sense that Jenn still fumed over having been trapped inside of the realm, even after the three hundred years or so that she had been in it.

She looked at him then and her expression suddenly changed. It was as if, after that discussion, seeing him made her realize his predicament. She reached out to touch his hands and said softly, lacking the hard edge to her voice. "I am so sorry, Aarvid. You may as well face up to it." She looked him straight in the eyes, and in that soft, emotional voice finished, "I have been avoiding this issue all day, Aarvid. For now, as long as you are in this realm, you will not be able to go back home, to your mother and sister."

"Never?" was his worried question. "You mean," he continued, his voice faltering, "I'll never see them again?"

"I did not mean that, Aarvid," she quickly interrupted. Worried, not wanting him to become more depressed, she continued, "Remember what I told you earlier? You will have the ability to go back and forth between realms at your own desire when you have learned to fully control the magic. Until then, you are stuck with me as your companion and we need to keep moving to try and stay ahead of our pursuers to be safe. They'll be after us until we decide to stop playing the game their way and find a way to beat them."

Stubbornly, he asked, "So, what's all this magic stuff got to do with me? Why can't I just help you get to a safe place and then use the magic to get back to home?"

Jenn was about to tell him about his father but, fearful of how he would react to that information especially after what he had done to that bug earlier, she decided to spare him that knowledge for now.

"Aarvid, if you know how to get back to your normal self, I give you permission to do so. Of course wait until we are on the ground, please."

"Gwaeeach," chimed in Gons. The big bird actually managed to sound a little worried.

"But, it will be no less dangerous for you," she continued. Then, more slowly, emphasizing each word, "It really is all about you, Aarvid!" Sighing deeply, "It has always been all about you, and those like you who had the potential to wield the magic, even before you discovered it by reading the book. True, they blame me for the mess I created for them. But, it's you they really are afraid of!"

It took Aarvid a few minutes to digest the information. Then he asked, "So, they are trying to get rid of me?" He raised his voice and sounded incredulous. "They want to kill me for being able to do a little magic? I thought they wanted me because they were perverts and wanted to kill you because you were helping me."

"Well, now you know. And, that little magic you mentioned…Do you realize what you did today? Do you think for one minute you could have done all that without using magic? Think about what you did to that poor bug, or never mind the bug. How about that poor fish that was suddenly forced to chomp on that creature whether it wanted to or not. In one big flash, that was more magic than I have ever felt in all my years here in the realm. Trouble is, now our pursuers know it too. They know that you have the potential to become the most powerful mage in the magic realm."

"Who will teach me how to use it then?" he asked, his face screwed up in a frown.

"Don't worry," she responded, hugging him then. "Just like what happened today, the lessons will come to you. I think." She tilted his head and looked into his eyes, "Just stay positive, Aarvid! If you can do that, everything will be all right. I'll be there to help you."

He hugged her back and, with a determined expression on his face, said, "I'll learn. I will become the strongest, and then…"

He left the sentence unfinished, because just then the big bird let out a loud and excited, "Gweeech!"

They both knew what it meant. They were at their destination.

CHAPTER 8
THE MAGIC TOME

The Cardinal was beside himself with anger. How could everybody be so incompetent? Until now his guardsmen had never let him down. Now, his most trusted henchman, Kirchner, was badly injured. He had failed his master and he would pay, he would pay dearly. Even David, his friend and most powerful mage in the realm, had let him down by separating himself, by taking his own path rather than working together as they had so often done in the past.

What to do next? He had to clear his head, rid himself of all distractions. *Remember*, he told himself, *I am on my own. I need to make sure that I can count on my magic to help me enter the real world and back again. David will not be there to bail me out when the magic fails me this time.* He crossed himself then, more to reassure himself than as a religious gesture and spoke a promise to himself. "I will have the magic tome when I am ready to return. I will have the power I need to rule here."

Finally, sounding pious, he added, "God willing all will be well when I am done."

He did not for a moment pause to consider what he might have to do to Mona, her mother, and possibly others to reacquire the Magic Tome and with it the magic he so coveted.

The newspaper reporter had been scanning the police log for the day looking for a filler story for tomorrow's edition. There it was. "…The disappearance of the young boy could possibly be explained as a kidnapping. The age of the younger sister makes her an unreliable witness…"

Was that not the sixth kidnapping of an underage child in less than a month? There was a real story here! Not just a filler.

Detective Rob VanderLinden, the local Interpol and Europol liason, picked up the phone. It was that pesky newspaper reporter from the Utrechtse Niews asking about another kidnapping. *What? Another kidnapping?* he asked himself. *Why wasn't I informed?*

"I am sorry, but I cannot share any details with you at this time," he told the reporter, adding, "Maybe later tonight or early tomorrow."

He scrambled to read the daily police log on his computer.

There it was. Who e-mailed that message into the log without sending him the complete report?

He had half a heart to call it a day and go home. Except, he had to have something to tell that pesky reporter and since his divorce, home was not that attractive an alternative any more.

May as well find out what it is all about, he told himself.

Constable Maartens had called it a day. All that commotion about that young boy with that hysterical mother and her lying little daughter had made him thirsty. Those kids were up to something. There was just no way that things could have happened the way that little girl had told him. He was certain that the youngster would show up shortly and all that commotion would be forgotten.

He had just downed one shot glass of Genever and felt the warm pleasurable burn sliding down his throat as he stretched his slippered feet out from his comfortable chair, when the phone rang.

"Maartens here…Yes, Detective…Interpol to be informed of all kidnappings?…Yes, Detective. I was just completing my report. Ehh, some of the details were a bit confusing…Yes, Detective. I'll be right here waiting for you…Yes, I know the family's address."

Cardinal Mephistopheles had reviewed his plan several times in his mind. Before starting his quest, out of habit, he kneeled in front of the small crucifix hanging on the wall of his temporary control center, asked for blessings, and crossed himself before getting up. He immediately moved over to his ornately carved chest, opened it, and pulled out a plain grey hooded monk's robe. He unfurled it. While holding the garment in front of him with both hands, he contemplated it fondly. Over the course of many centuries, he had had many adventures in that robe. All of them had taken place outside the magic realm, in the real world where he had very limited powers. This time would be different, he would have the tome. It would enhance his magic to rival David's.

Just thinking of having that kind of power warmed his soul. Yes, there would be nothing he would not do to have it. After all, God had willed it so. He had given it to him and David to be its caretakers. It was his duty to take it back!

Thus, dressed in the plain robes of a monk, Cardinal Mephistopheles set out to take back the Magic Tome.

It was during the darkness of the early evening that the Cardinal, wearing a plain monk's garb, found himself crossing the bridge over the canal near the house in which, as he had been told, the Rocher family lived. There was not a single soul around to observe the strange apparition presented by the cardinal, a Monk's dark brown, hooded outfit draped around his hulking frame. No one saw him as he placed himself on he far side of the narrow, tree lined country road in front of the small cottage. Nearly invisible in the moonless darkness, he mumbled the magic phrases that brought to live the fire that would surely consume the cottage and its inhabitants. The book would remain unharmed, protected as it was by its own magic. Soon, he would be in possession of it once more.

He felt alive with excitement. The anticipation was almost too great to bear. He could not remember the last time he had felt this alive. Well, maybe it was akin to how he had felt several centuries ago when he had watched that young, French peasant girl burn at the stake in fire he had created. What had been her name? He could not remember right now. Wasn't it Jean or something?

He was not really trying to remember, but somehow the memory just came to him. Her name had been Jean D'Arc. Her image flashed clearly in his mind's eye and with it the powerful emotions that had buoyed him then. With an effort he pushed the memory and the accompanying apprehension aside.

He had to really focus on his task. A task that would be much more difficult for him to accomplish out of the magic realm. Intently he watched as the magic fire ball in his hand grew from a tiny glimmer to a large fiery sphere.

Inside the house, all appeared quiet and dark.

Deliberately he reached back, his hand filled with the fiery magic, and heaved.

The fireball traveled rapidly through the intervening space. It entered one of the large front windows and, to his horror, excited the house, continued on, and struck the shed behind the neighboring home. Instantly, it was engulfed in flames that lit up the whole area.

Suddenly, he was not as confident any more. Could the magic book have a protection spell over the whole house? If so, he would probably be unable to return to the magic realm. He would be in real trouble. Shaking visibly now, he redoubled his efforts at creating a new fireball.

Mom! Slightly worried at her mother's lack of response, Mona pushed herself away from her mother's tight embrace. Mom! She tried to shake her mother out of her tear filled stupor without success. Finally, she got up and in the darkened home walked carefully to where the phone continued to ring.

It was Detective Vander Linden. He asked if Mona was all right and if he could speak to Mona's mother.

Mona carried the phone to her mother and pressed it to her ear. Gemma responded by holding the phone herself. She nodded and answered in the affirmative several times, sniffling, and rubbing tears from her eyes. The phone call appeared to have pulled her out of her stupor, at least temporarily.

Looking at Mona with her wet and red-rimmed eyes, she said, "A detective is coming to investigate. He says he is from Interpol or Europol and charged with investigating disappearances of underage children." After retrieving tissues to wipe her eyes and noisily clear her nose, she sounded hopeful when she continued, speaking more to herself than to her daughter, "He says he is very concerned and will come as fast as he can. Maybe he will come up with something…"

"But, Mom!" Mona loudly interrupted her mother's ramblings, sounding very put out. "Doesn't anybody listen to me? Didn't you hear me when I told you? Aarvid disappeared just like that!" She slapped her hands together to emphasize the point.

"Poof, and he was gone! He was mumbling something! It must have been this Magic Book! Maybe he is inside of it. I tell you, Mom, it was magic!" Mona sounded so convinced it took Gemma aback.

For a moment she was speechless as she watched her daughter pick up something from right next to her on the sofa and place it in her lap. To Gemma it looked large and heavy, but it was not. "You mean that? It looks like a very heavy book." She thought it strange that she had not noticed it before now.

Mona could not believe what she was hearing. Her mother actually saw the book! "Yes," she confirmed excited, while settling next to her mother and leaning into her. With both hands placed on the tome for emphasis, Mona spoke rapidly and in an excited voice, "This is the book Aarvid was reading when he disappeared. And, it is not heavy. See?" She was holding the tome in both hands, ready to present it to her mother once again, when all of a sudden it felt warm in her hands and started vibrating slightly. Alarmed, Mona jumped up and felt the book pull her about so that she faced the front window.

The large fireball that flashed through the front window and headed right for them startled her so much that all she could do was to hold the book in front of her to shield herself and her mother. With eyes that were too startled to blink, she observed the fireball approach rapidly, take a sudden turn that took it out through the rear door, and finally explode in a fiery explosion somewhere in the yard next door.

"What…?" was all Gemma could stammer out.

"I don't know," mumbled Mona. As if in a trance, she walked rapidly to the large window where the fireball had entered and looked out, firmly hanging onto the tome with both hands.

Outside the darkness was lit up by the fiery conflagration next door. Still, at first she observed nothing out of the ordinary. Then, she saw the large, dark shape across the street as it shifted and moved closer. In its hand, stretched in front of its monstrous face, it carried another tiny ball of fire. To her consternation, the little fireball in his hand was growing bigger and bigger.

"Mom!" She could barely speak as the realization hit her. "There is somebody out there! He is going to throw that thing!"

Fear close to panic gripped her. Mona felt as if her feet were nailed to the floor. She saw the creature's face clearly when he brought the ball of fire to his face to inspect it. It was a grotesque human face, dark grey, with pronounced ridges where eyebrows would be, and a heavy square jaw with jowls. It was the eyes that really spooked her; they were slitted like those of a crocodile and glowed reddish in the yellow glow of the slowly growing fireball.

The creature outside stretched himself to his full height as he reared back with the hand containing the fireball. He was huge! Mona had never seen anyone that size. Just as he brought the lumbering arm forward to release his missile, Mona heard her mother behind her asking, "What is going on out…*gasp*!"

Gemma was brought up short by the sight of the fireball coming straight at them. She wanted to jump forward and pull Mona down from in front of the large window, but her legs would not obey. Instead she raised both her arms to shield her face and protect herself. She could not miss the silent form of her daughter standing in front of the window, outlined against the light of the fiery projectile that was about to slam into her.

Mona felt the slight vibration in the tome at about the same time she heard her mother approach. The warmth of the tome and the slight vibration reminded her of the previous incident. All sense of fear left her. She felt completely calm. She knew what she must do.

Mona raised the Magic Tome with both of her hands, placing it in the exact path of the approaching fireball. All she meant to do was block it, as she somehow knew it would. Instead, she was surprised to see the fireball harmlessly bounce off the flat surface of the tome and…head straight back at the hulking figure standing in the lane in front of the house.

It had taken the Cardinal precious seconds to create his second fireball, something that would be almost instantaneous inside the magic realm. He reared back and hurled it, aiming the fiery object at the roof of the house. He was surprised to see it curve downward, heading straight toward the front window instead. For a split second, he saw her, outlined by the light, standing in front of the window inside the house, with the book held out in front of her.

In the next instant, the fireball bounced of the tome and accelerated right back at him. It was all he could do to mumble deflective phrases and jump clear of the fiery object's path. With a whoosh it passed by him, close enough to singe all the hair on his face. Next, it exploded against the trunk of the nearest tree and instantly set it ablaze. In the following instant, he realized that he was on fire as well and, with a yammering howl, hurtled himself onto the ground.

After making certain that he had snuffed the flames that had consumed a part of his robe, he hurriedly made off, across the bridge, in the direction of the old windmill.

Mephistopheles felt panicked. So far, nothing had gone the way he had expected things to go. Not with the boy, nor now with the girl. As he hurried along the dark road, David's words rang clearly through his mind. *...The tome has the ability to choose who wields the magic. Maybe it even manipulates events to cause this to happen. It may have happened already!...The young boy and his sister?*

He needed time to think, time to get his wits together. How was he going to accomplish that running along these dark roads, worrying about getting away, like some hunted criminal?

Mephistopheles stopped and looked around. The sky above was dark; cloud cover obscured the moon and the stars. Ahead, the darkness was impenetrable, while behind him the raging inferno. He could sense the old windmill not too far in the distance. He would go there and focus all his efforts on getting back to the security of the magic realm.

The darkness was pierced by the approaching dual lights of a car. He knew he was close to the old structure because he could hear the creaking of the old wooden wings in the wind, interrupted by the occasional flapping of a loose piece of canvass. Thus distracted, in a hurry to reach it, he forgot about the pond in front of the structure.

With a loud splash he received a very wet reminder; picking himself up in the hip deep water, he was totally soaked. He snorted loudly to clear his airways and angrily wiped the water from his face. He discovered then that it was impossible for him to move because his boots had sunk deeply into the soft mud of the pond's bottom. He tried desperately and unsuccessfully to get his booted feet free. The bright lights of the approaching car punctuated the urgency of his situation.

He had just managed to pull one foot out of its mud-anchored boot, when the car came around the last turn in the road, its twin lights swinging around to illuminate him directly. Mephistopheles had no choice but to submerge himself almost completely, hoping that the few rushes along the edge would hide his partially submerged head sufficiently.

The affront to his self esteem angered him but not enough to overcome his fear of being found out. He had been in jail once before, more than seven hundred years ago and that had almost cost him his life. He had a deadly fear of losing control like that again. Come to think about it, he had little control over his situation at this time and he did not like it one bit. He wished he had possession of the power of the magic. He would have torched that loud and obnoxious piece of metal with its occupants into a small puddle of molten metal and carbon dust before making his grand return into the magic realm. Instead, here he was cowering in the cold water and blowing bubbles. He mumbled the words of the spell that would return him to the realm. When nothing happened, his spirits dipped even lower; he was close to being desperate, but not quite there. Not him, the scourge of the Magic Realm for whom thousands trembled in fear.

Spitting out water, he mumbled, "The Lord has forsaken me. Just like Job."

Detective Vanderlinden and Constable Maartens were rapidly approaching the old mill. The detective had wanted to get a look at the scene of the disappearance before proceeding to interview the mother and her daughter one more time. The silence that had reigned during their short ride was broken by Maartens when he said, "We are here. It was inside this old mill the young girl said her brother supposedly disappeared." The constable had slowed and was turning into what once had been the access to the property, when the detective spoke with a suddenness and alarm that made him bring the car to a sudden grinding halt.

"What is happening over there?!" VanderLinden was pointing down the road. "Down there a ways, on the other side of the canal. What is out there? It looks like a fire!"

When Maartens finally managed to turn his rotund body around to look, he saw it too. Immediately, he felt his stomach knot. He did not need to guess where the fire was. "It's at their house." He emphasized the *their*. "It's where the mother and her daughter live, where the disappeared youngster lives."

"Well, what are we still sitting here for?" was the annoyed question. "Get to it, man! Get going so that we can get to the house! Something must have happened out there!"

Tires skidding on dirt and squealing onto pavement, Maartens accelerated down the road toward the house.

With more than a little effort, the Cardinal managed to liberate his soaked and cold body from the sticky ooze of the pond bottom and get back to dry land. Barefoot and dripping volumes of water from the heavy wool garment that weighed down on his large shoulders, he spat out the remains of pond water from mouth and nostrils and grumbled, "When I get back to the realm, someone is going to wish they were in hell before I am done with them!" While trying to shake the water out of his dripping garments, he growled, "Kirchner, you may yet wish that that young boy had finished you off!"

Grumbling and promising death and worse on his subjects, he stumbled blindly toward the old windmill.

Judging from the creaking sounds, he was nearly there when he heard the wailing sound of an approaching fire engine. He was in such a hurry to get inside the windmill and so intent on not ending up in the water again that he did not pay enough attention to the structure that suddenly appeared right in front of him. Thus, as his stretched out arm passed through the gap of the nearly half opened door, his face made solid contact with the doorjamb. For the first time since he had been a young man, Mephistopheles swore loudly and more than once. While checking his bloodied upper lip and teeth, he entered the silent, tomblike darkness within. Blindly, he took a couple of steps, hurried on by the rapidly approaching sound of the fire engine. Instantly, he was made to pay for his haste. As his bare feet stepped on the sharp pebbles of stone that littered the floor, he tripped, stumbling headlong into the millstone and the heavy wooden beam leaning across it. His forehead hit the beam so hard that he would have passed out if it had not been for the excruciating pain from his shin as it bounced off the remains of the grinding stone.

As he picked himself off the dusty floor, he did not even notice the small cuts and scrapes he gained on his hands by leaning on them. Groggily, hanging on with one hand to anything within reach, he touched his throbbing forehead with the other. Blood was flowing from a large rapidly growing lump; some of it entered his eyes as he unwittingly smeared blood all over his face, stinging them as well.

Swaying in place he stood there, momentarily unable to go on, head and shin throbbing with pain, blood stinging his eyes, and tasting the salty blood from his swollen and split lip. Unfortunately for Mephistopheles, when the fire engine passed by and temporarily bathed parts of the interior in light, he had his eyes closed trying to clear the blood from them by wiping them with his moist garment. So it was that he did not see the other obstacles waiting for him as he was trying to make his way to what he desperately hoped would be the safety of the small back room.

When the detective and the constable arrived at her home, Gemma had already dialed the emergency number for the nearest fire station and the local constabulary. Constable DeGroot, who had the night's duty, had informed her that he would be on his way and not to worry, because Constable Maartens should be nearly there.

Gemma was more than a little confused. With all that had been happening today and with Mona close to convincing her that there was some sort of magic that was causing it all to happen, her head was literally spinning. Thus, when Detective VanderLinden and Constable Maartens pulled up, she hardly noticed them. She stood outside her home, clinging to Mona almost as much for her own support as to succor her daughter's emotional upset, staring at the fire across the lane that by now had engulfed two trees.

Rob VanderLinden saw them standing in the middle of the small front yard, hugging one another and looking up at the blaze that was rapidly consuming two large trees. On the way to the house, Maartens had quickly provided some basic details about the family. He had not forgotten to include the fact that her husband had died by fire under suspicious circumstances some years ago. Seeing the fire and the vulnerable woman and child, it struck the detective that this was too coincidental. *Fire is threatening this family again? Hmm...It could be just circumstance, but I do not think so. I'll have to be alert to pick up some clues.*

As he walked over to the clinging couple, he could not help but notice that she was a very good looking woman. For a moment he forgot himself and stared openly.

When Gemma finally realized that two gentlemen were

walking toward her through the open gate, she turned to face them. Constable Maartens was busy looking at the flames leaping from the treetops but the tall stranger accompanying him was intently staring at her. She realized that she must look absolutely dreadful. Letting go of Mona, she quickly wiped her eyes and face with the sleeve of her blouse and smiled perfunctorily.

The detective did not wait for Maartens to introduce him, instead he walked straight up to Gemma and introduced himself softly and expressed regret for what had happened. Almost immediately while his eyes took in the young girl next to her mother, he inquired, "What happened? What caused this fire?"

He had expected the mother to answer. Instead, it was the beautiful child with her unruly crop of auburn hair and soft hazel eyes that answered, "Hi, are you the detective from intropol?" She reached out her small hand and said, "I'm Mona and this is my mom." Looking him straight in the eyes she continued, "A huge monster man made magic fire balls and threw them at us. This magic Tome…" she pointed at something she was holding with her other hand, "…saved us. He ran off that way, down the road." She pointed in the direction from which they had just come.

Maartens, who had joined them, asked in a skeptical tone, "Is that right, madam?"

Hearing it, Detective VanderLinden was thinking, *He is challenging the evidence presented by an eyewitness, putting her in the defensive. We did not see anyone on that road but that does not mean anything. Something must be hiding out there.* When he looked at the disheveled pair in front of him, another thought struck him. *They must both be exhausted, yet still they both have great looks, and that widow is extremely attractive.*

If that boy had their looks… He did not dare finish the thought. Instead he asked, looking at Gemma, "Your boy, how old is he?"

Gemma looked at the detective as if seeing him for the first time. She remembered his first name being Rob. He was taller than Maartens, with a pleasant, clean-shaven face crowned by neatly trimmed dark brown hair. He made it seem as if Aarvid was right inside, waiting for her. "He is just short of twelve. Tall for his age and…" She was going to say, *Not at all the kind of boy who would do anything that would take him away from his home.* Instead, she busied herself, wiping the new tears that had come to her eyes.

Rob VanderLinden had the urge to hold her and console her. Instead he touched her hand lightly, patted it and said, "If there is any way he can be found, I will find it and…" looking at Mona and stroking her fluffy crop, "…I promise I will, even if I have to deal with magic and evil people." He looked back at Gemma and asked, "Can we go inside to talk? I would also appreciate a picture of your son to take with me to distribute."

Gemma nodded silently. They had all started toward the front door when the detective suddenly stopped and spoke to Maartens, "Oh, Constable. Could you please investigate the possible arsonist? I recommend looking inside that old windmill if nothing turns up on the roads. Please advise Constable DeGroot to meet you there. I'll join you there as well after I am done here." He turned and rejoined mother and daughter who were on their way into their home. He was surprised when Mona grabbed his hand and hugged it tightly to her chest and against the bundle she was holding.

They were in their living room. Gemma had reached over to take a picture form on top of one of the small cabinets that decorated the room and turned to face the detective, ready to hand him the picture.

The detective had found Mona still clinging to his arm and looking up at him. He turned to her and half squatted to be eye level with her. It was then, that he discovered that the object she was holding was an ornately bound book. He was surprised that he had not noticed it until now. Mona relaxed when she saw that he had noticed the book and let go of his arm. Rob placed both arms on her shoulders and asked concerned, "Eh, Mona…are you all right? You were terribly frightened. Weren't you?" He felt like he was going to say something else while she nodded in the affirmative. He felt slightly confused. Wasn't there something else? It was almost as if something was redirecting his attention.

With a serious expression, her eyes large and intent on him, she seemed to be holding something to her chest, and she was speaking to him. "…the only one who believed me right away. No one else believed me when I told them Aarvid disappeared with magic and the monster man used magic fireballs. You are the only one to see the book, the book of magic." Again, she took his hand and pressed it to her chest and the package.

The detective was dumbfounded. There it was. It was that ornately bound book. He had to touch it to see it and if he released it, it would direct his attention elsewhere. In his mind it registered, *A book of magic?* His spoken question was, "Where did you get this book, Mona?"

He ended up sitting cross-legged on the ground with her sitting in front of him while he kept his hand on the book as it was lying on her crossed legs. All the while Mona told her tale of how Aarvid had suddenly gone up in thin air, of the strange feeling she had when the large white swan flew over their heads, and of course how this magic book had saved their lives when the Monster Man with the crocodile eyes tried burning them with magic fireballs. Detective Rob VanderLinden did not know what to believe. One thing was for certain, he was not going to dismiss what she had just told him with all the sincerity of an innocent nine-year-old.

Gemma had sat herself down, picture in hand, and observed the way the detective seemed to take everything that Mona told him very seriously. He also had a way about him that she found very likeable; the way he interacted with her and Mona conveyed an understanding of their pain and frustration. She could not help listening to her daughter as she emphatically kept referring to a book and how it somehow played a major role in all that had happened. Yet, every time she tried to remember what book that was she ended up distracted. Instead, most of the time she found herself preoccupied, wandering about this Rob VanderLinden.

Finally, the detective turned to her, reached out and asked if he could have the picture. He looked at it, pursed his lips, looked her in the eyes, and with a gentle voice said, "Mrs. Rocher, you have two extremely handsome children." Getting up, he reached out to her hand, held it for a moment and reiterated what he had just promised Mona. "If there is a way to return your son, Aarvid, to you safely, I will find it. Until such time as I can get back to you, please get some rest. I promise I'll do what I can." Turning back to where Mona was seated, he smiled to her and gently touched her hair as he admonished, "You, too, young lady! Off to bed!"

It was just then that the fire engine arrived. Holding both hands palms out toward them as they had both gotten up to follow him on the way to the front door, he pleaded, "Please, go get some rest. I'll talk to the fire crew. They'll have the fire under control and out before you get to sleep."

Heading toward the door he added, "Please lock all the doors. I'll check the road on my way to meet up with the two constables. Someone will regularly drive by to check things out. Now, please have a restful night." With that, he let himself out the door and was gone.

The Cardinal was just picking himself off the ground in the small back room. Ever since he had entered the old structure it had been one big booby-trap. He was bloodied from his encounter with the millstone, bruised from falling over broken wall board, and cut on his hands, feet, and behind from stepping on broken bottles and then falling on those and other shards. Outside he could hear a car pulling into the access, its lights temporarily illuminating all the obstacles he had tangled with. What could he do now? He wanted to howl out his frustration. He was angry and at the same time scared out of his wits. He was out of options.

At wit's end, he decided that maybe it would not hurt to do what he had not done for a very long time. He dared not to kneel. So, standing in place he crossed himself and prayed. The cardinal was amazed at how good it felt.

...and I promise I will not willfully revenge myself on those inside the magic realm who are incapable of fending off my wrath and... He had just completed making that promise as part of his prayer, when the painfully bright beam of a flashlight hit him squarely in the face. Even interrupted, the prayer had allowed him to reach a quiet place in his mind, to put aside the burning pain of his cuts and bruises, as well as the all consuming fear that had obsessed him. Opening his eyes slowly into the bright light, he mumbled the words of the spell.

The two constables had proceeded slowly from the house, checking both areas along the road that could conceivably be hiding someone. They had finally arrived at the towering structure of the old, cursed wind mill. As they checked out the area around the mill they had noticed the area where the vegetation bordering the pond had been crushed by a large, wet person or creature. The wet trail had led directly to the half open door leading into the old structure.

Maartens pushed against the door, slowly opening it wider, so that he could check its interior. From behind him, Constable DeGroot had raised his flashlight over Maartens' head to provide additional illumination. Together, the two lights provided enough light for Maartens to see the large wet prints lead directly toward the large broken millstone and the large beam leaning onto it. After examining the rough edged stone closely, he noticed droplets of blood on the dirt strewn floor.

The two constables followed the tracks and bloody trail into the back of the mill. They led toward the small back room.

Maartens wished then that he had remembered to bring his Billy club. Afraid to show the nervous tick in his right eyelid to his companion, he continued to lead his partner and followed the trail over and through obstacles. With his knees shaking violently, he headed directly toward the door leading to the back room.

Carefully, Maartens opened the nearly closed door. His flashlight made an arc as it swung slowly around with the door. Then, there it was. Illuminated by the beam of his light the giant, hooded creature stood unmoving near the back of the room. In a slow, deliberate fashion, it pulled apart the two massive hands that had been clasped in prayer-like fashion under its huge, carved and squared chin. What made the blood drain from Maartens' brain were the two orange, glowing reptilian eyes that opened, equally deliberate, from the cavernous, shadowed depths underneath large, bridged eyebrows and were separated by an impressive, bulbous nose.

With an audible sigh Maartens collapsed to the floor.

Constable DeGroot had been ill at ease throughout this expedition into the dark confines of the cursed Mill. He had stayed so close to Maartens that he had needed to be careful not to step on his heels as they carefully made their way to the back with darkness closing in all around him. He had been ill prepared to come face to face with the creature inside, even with Maartens between himself and it.

When Maartens inexplicably collapsed, it was too much for DeGroot. Dropping his flashlight, he panicked and dashed heedlessly back, toward the doorway that stood illuminated by the car's headlight, in the process, running into obstacles and painfully injuring his shinbones.

He had sat inside the car for just a few minutes, desperately trying to slow his rapid breathing, pounding heart, and gather his wits, when a rap on the car windshield almost made him jump out of the car seat. DeGroot did not know whether he was going to put the car in gear and drive off with the accelerator pressed all the way to the floor, or look up to see who, or what was outside his car window. Fortunately, before impulse became action, he recognized the voice that called to him as belonging to Detective VanderLinden. "Constable, what is going on? Where is Constable Maartens?"

Constable DeGroot took a few gulps of air while he lowered his window and answered, still slightly out of breath, "Uhh...I think he is dead! *Gasp*...I think the creature inside there..." he nodded toward the open door of the mill, "I think it killed him with its red-orange laser eyes. It was just awful!"

"Well, where is that creature now?" the detective asked, concern mixing with the excitement in his voice. Before the constable had a chance to answer, he followed it up with, "My God! You left Maartens all alone inside there?"

Detective Vanderlinden started for the door, fumbling in his pocket for his small penlight and quickly touching the reassuring comfort of the small hard bundle made by his service revolver, tucked under his left armpit. With the small light adding little light to the already well lit scene, he entered into the much darker interior, followed closely by the constable.

The detective had barely started to advance carefully toward the abandoned lights that partially illuminated the backroom, when a dark shape slowly rose in front of him. *"Gasp!* It is the creature!"* The barely audible whisper escaped from DeGroot, as he tried to pull the detective back with him by grabbing and tugging on the back of his jacket.

With his left hand holding his penlight stretched out in front of him, and his right cradling his small weapon, half out of its holster, Rob VanderLinden pressed forward until the tiny beam of his light illuminated the confused and startled face of Constable Maartens.

Wide eyed, unsteady and frightened, Maartens blinked a few times into the narrow beam. He perked up visibly when he heard a voice say, "Thank God you are all right, Maartens!" In the next instant it all came back to him, he remembered where he was and what had caused him to black out. Still not too steady, he fumbled around on the dark floor for the dropped flashlight while his eyes desperately searched in the dark shadows for anything that could indicate the presence of the creature. Rocking the light wildly back and forth, he finally steadied it and aimed at an empty area in the back of the small room. With the others now standing to either side of him, he mumbled, "Bless the good Lord! He is gone!"

All that remained to indicate someone had been there was a large area of wetness. There were prints leading up to the spot, but none going away in any direction. Whomever or whatever it was that had been there had totally vanished.

Detective VanderLinden picked up the second discarded flashlight and followed the prints carefully to the area of puddled wetness. He stooped down several times to check, rubbing his finger into the dark stains and checking it out each time under the light. "Hmm," he whispered almost more to himself than to his audience, "so it bleeds just like any of us, but he or it can disappear into thin air. Just like the boy did." He stood there looking at the irregular ring of moisture and carefully checked the area around it once more, all the while rubbing his short, brown hair. He looked puzzled.

"So, now that you've had a few moments to think about it, what do you think about this?" He had turned to look at Maartens, but gave DeGroot a quick glance as well.

The constable fumbled around for words. He had no explanation. Until his face to face meeting with what he called "The Creature," he had totally dismissed all that nonsense about magic. Now, standing inside this dark ominous structure, he was reluctant to admit it verbally, but in reality he was totally spooked. This was definitely not business as usual.

When neither one of the constables managed to say anything meaningful, the detective asked the question that was burning on his mind. "OK. Now, what do you think might have happened to the boy?"

"I am sure of one thing! Somehow, that creature is tied into it somehow," Maartens responded thoughtfully.

Constable DeGroot just stood there shaking his head while his eyes kept flitting about, just in case.

The tall detective stood there for another few moments saying nothing, looking first at one constable then at the other and finally back at the empty space above the still very wet floor. Finally, still scratching his head, he said, "I wish I knew what the HELL was going on here. One thing is for certain. You are right about that…eh, whatever it is, being part of the puzzle. One thing we did learn, and that is that we have to take little Mona's testimony very serious." As he completed his statement, he headed for the bright lights illuminating the doorway and the car sitting idle in the driveway beyond that.

After completing his report and checking his messages, Detective Rob Vanderlinden stood at his desk for several minutes just staring into space. Finally, he seemed to have come to a decision.

Nearly two hours after he had interviewed the mother and her daughter, he was back at their house, parked his comfortable, mid-sized car off the road in front of the house, and tried to get some sleep himself.

CHAPTER 9
MONA'S MAGIC

It was a dark night. The moon and stars were prevented from relieving the oppressive darkness by an invisible blanket of clouds. Yet Aarvid could make out the soft feathery outline of their makeshift shelter.

Pushed into the muddy side of the old nest and placed in an overlapping manner, the curved feathers created a small dome. They formed a perfect barrier against wind and weather. Against that backdrop, he could see Jenn feeling her way around her side of the cozy space preparing her own place to bed down. Outside he could hear the soft sighing sound of the smooth waves wearing themselves out amongst the reeds and rushes that surrounded the elevated nest in which they had built their shelter. Occasionally, the humming song of the wind, stroking the myriad stalks of vegetation and marsh grass, would intrude on the many other unusual sounds he could hear as he was lying in his bed of small downy feathers.

He felt more relaxed after the discussion they had while they were still flying. Now that he'd had time to let it sink in, more questions inundated his mind. He did not know where to begin, so he started by summarizing. "So, they want to control the magic? That's all? They think I am dangerous because I can do magic?" As he spoke those words, something tickled his mind. It was almost as if someone was there listening in on their conversation.

There was no response from Jenn. Maybe, she too had felt that slight brush against her mind. When she continued to tuck and stuff downy feathers into the space meant for her to lie down in, he continued, "What if I can convince them that they can have it all, that I do not want any part of the magic?"

He watched her stop what she had been doing, heard her sigh deeply, and sit down on her incomplete bed. She knew who he meant by "them." For a few moments she quietly stared in his direction before she spoke. "Aarvid, remember what I asked of you earlier, to trust me?"

When he grunted in the affirmative, she continued, "There are some things I will share with you in due time. For now, please believe me when I tell you that it won't make any difference what you tell them. They don't care what your intentions are with regards to the use of your magic. All you need to realize is that they consider you a threat. From what I have learned after all these years about Cardinal Mephistopheles, as well as the Black Mage David, is that they do not take any threat to their control of the magic lightly. You are a potent threat to them and I really believe that they will only be satisfied when you have been eliminated. You will have to go on believing that until such time as one or both prove me wrong. The only thing that will change my mind, and hopefully yours, is through their actions."

Aarvid felt the emptiness close in on him as he listened. It seemed darker somehow. He felt very vulnerable. How was he going to fend off two powerful magic beings all by himself? If they ever caught up with Jenn and him, how would he be able to keep both of them safe? It seemed all so unfair. In his mind he told himself, *I am just a kid. I don't understand all that happened today. What if tomorrow I forget how I somehow managed to do it all? ...I want to go home.*

He did not speak his thoughts out loudly. He just sighed, got up from his bedding and walked over to where he could barely make out Jenn's outline. He sat down close to her, leaned against her and put his head against her shoulder. He sounded very lost and tired when he said, "I miss my mom and my pesky little sister. I wish I was back home."

He wiped a tear from his eye and continued, "Maybe this is all just a bad dream and tomorrow when I wake up, everything will be back to the way it was."

He did not expect the hug he received, but it did feel nice and comforting.

With his head now cradled in the hollow under her chin, she stroked the back of his head before pulling it backward enough to allow her to lean her forehead against his.

"Aarvid, believe me, I wish it did not have to be this way." She spoke very softly, her voice stroking him tenderly. "We're in this together. For better or worse, let's make the best of it and see where this road takes us." She was quiet for the few moments it took her to turn back to face in the direction she had been when he had leaned his head against her shoulder. Then, with a deep sigh, she continued pensively, "You can't turn the clock back, Aarvid. We need to move on. I need you to be strong."

"OK…I'll try," he responded barely audible, while getting up to return to his bed.

He laid there, his eyes opened wide and his senses alert to anything. He could still feel the presence of someone. For some reason that "almost presence" that touched his mind made him feel very homesick; it felt like he could almost touch his sister, as if she was sitting right there next to him. Then, just as sudden it was gone. Slowly, he allowed himself to relax.

Jenn felt terrible doubts assailing her as she listened to him sigh deeply before turning to get comfortable. He was just a babe, so young. *Did I make the terrible mistake that my father accused me of, or have I really saved this child from a more terrible fate?* Once again he sighed deeply. *What could be more terrible than to be separated from his home and his mother and sister? What right have I to have made that choice for him?*

On the other side of the tent Aarvid's breathing seemed more relaxed. *He must be going to sleep.* His rhythmic breathing seemed to relax her as well. *After all, he did do incredible things today. He certainly proved that his abilities and his inner strengths were formidable.*

Just before dosing off to sleep, she reminded herself that most of what had happened today seemed to have been out of her control. She was giving herself way too much credit. Something else was pulling the threads. They were just the puppets. She just wished she had a better idea who, or what was the puppeteer.

"Mona, where are you?" She could hear his voice clearly. The room looked just like it had when they had visited it earlier that day. On the workbench she could clearly discern the book of magic. Its pages were still flipping about, when his voice echoed through her brain, rattling her nerves once again, "Please, stop playing this silly game! You're scaring me! Why can't you see me?"

She felt the fear all over again, that numbing fear of not knowing what happened. Woodenly she walked over to the workbench and closed the tome and hugged it to her body. However, it grew hot and vibrated in her hands. She held it out in front of her and then she saw him. She was no longer in that small back room inside the old mill. She stood in her front window, panic roiling inside her stomach, facing that horrible creature. She could see him more clearly than she had before. His face, half hidden under the shadows of the deep cowl that covered his head, was distorted by a malicious toothy grimace that was surrounded by deep gray folds of skin. The unnaturally textured folds were split by a huge, prominent nose. These same folds of blotchy, grey skin supported two, bright orange, glowing snake eyes. They stared at her unblinking from beneath two dominating folds that once could have been eyebrows. The huge maw of a jaw opened and from its dark pink interior, issued a deep growl. Next, in a low throaty roar it screamed, "Give it to me! It is mine! It is my divine gift! Give me THAT BOOK!" Those terrible red glowing eyes stared at her in a hypnotizing way. Mona felt herself being drawn into them. Instinctively, she raised the book to shield herself from those eyes. It worked, she felt balanced once again.

The creature roared, raising its hands skyward. Then, it reared back and heaved a fiery projectile. A ball of writhing flames headed straight for her, growing larger and larger until it was large enough to consume her. She wanted to scream, but could not because she realized that she had been holding her breath all that time. In desperation, she brought up the small magic tome. Amazed, she observed the blazing inferno that was all around her sucked into the small book.

She sagged down to the carpet, marveling at the book she was holding in both her hands, and sighed deeply. It was more beautiful than ever; its colors virtually glowed red, black and gold. Silently admiring it, she stroked it with one hand and noticed the red glow of the copper band on one of her fingers as she stroked the beautiful, soft cover.

The colors just seemed to dim a little, but as she continued to stroke the tome a mist formed over its surface. In the mist a picture formed. At first, it was not well defined, but soon she recognized who it was. It was her brother, still wearing nothing but his swimming trunks. He was filthy, sitting amongst tufts of downy feathers of the purest white. Next to him sat a young woman. Underneath the layer of dirt that covered her, Mona could tell that she was beautiful.

They must have been flying; there were fluffy clouds in the pure blue sky behind them. Suddenly, the bird veered off, downward away from her. For just a few seconds, she had an attack of vertigo caused by the realization that she was maybe a thousand feet up in the air. She watched as the large white bird…No, it was a white swan…It was THE white swan!…She watched as it slowly grew smaller, heading down, toward a small island surrounded by blue water.

She did not want to look down because it made her dizzy, so she rotated her body around, and…She was on a narrow stretch of beach. Aarvid sat just a few feet away from her, his head buried between his knees. Mona walked over to him, placed her small hand lightly on his now clean shoulder and tried pulling him out from between those tucked-up knees. She heard herself saying, "Aarvid, let's go home. Mom is worried sick about you."

Aarvid lifted his head up to face her. He had been crying; tears were still clinging to his cheeks. He reached out his hand toward her. Her brother looked dreadfully tired and all scratched up, but he was here next to her, alive. Temporarily relieved, she took his hand in hers and, feeling him get up from the sand, turned around to pull him with her…She was back in her room holding onto nothing but a thick tome.

Desperately she searched, sweeping the room with her eyes. Her brother was nowhere to be seen; she had lost him again.

When the knot returned to her stomach and with it the fear, Mona woke up and found herself clinging to her blankets, drenched in sweat.

"Mom!" Her shrill cry echoed through the house. "Mom! I saw him!"

It seemed like she'd just fallen asleep when the piercing scream of Mona awoke her. In an instant Gemma was in her daughter's room.

Mona sat on the edge of her bed, still clinging to her blankets. Her usually fluffy hair was matted and perspiration covered her small body.

Kneeling in front of her teary eyed daughter, she caressed her, gently asking, "What is the matter, dear?" Gently, she lifted the delicate face by the chin so she could look into those large round eyes and pleaded, "Mona, what is the matter, dear? Please tell me so that I can help you."

"You can't, Mom!" Mona blurted out between tears. "It's magic, real magic!"

Gemma was about to sit down on the bed next to her daughter, when they were both startled by loud pounding on the front door. As Gemma rushed to the door, she was reassured by hearing the detective's voice, "Is everything all right inside?"

Rob VanderLinden stopped pounding on the door only after he heard her voice tell him that all was OK, and to wait just a minute so that she could unlock the door and open it.

Gemma opened the door and was slightly bemused by the

spectacle he presented. Wearing a concerned look on his sleep creased face; the detective was still breathing hard from his sprint to the front door and looked thoroughly disheveled. It looked like he had dressed himself during his impromptu run. He wore no jacket and his rumpled shirt hung half out of his pants. The right pant leg, hung up on his black sock, was halfway up his calf. Neither foot was completely inside the loafers he was wearing. He had obviously woken up with a start at hearing Mona's shouting and made a beeline straight for the front door, not even bothering to shut his car door.

When Gemma entered, accompanied by the rumpled and concerned-looking detective, Mona was seated on her bed with her legs folded under of her.

"I think Mona was about to share something important with me," she said upon entering. "Isn't that right, dear?"

Mona looked at them impatiently and nodded. She seemed to have regained her composure during the brief interlude.

"Mom, sit here!" she insisted, pointing at one side next to her on the bed. Smiling expectantly at the detective while indicating her other side, she added, "Hi, you can sit over here."

Once they had placed themselves on either side of her, Mona continued, wide awake and in an excited voice, "I was dreaming, but it was real, Mom; really, it was real! And, I saw Aarvid. He was flying on the back of that swan. You know, Mom? It was the same one we saw flying by us near the windmill. There was a young woman with him…I also saw that creature man. You know the one that threw the fire balls!…He is really scary!"

Mona turned and looked up at them then, first at her mom, who had protectively surrounded her with her arm, and then at the detective, whose sleep creased face took her in compassionately. When they seemed to be waiting for her to continue, she reached out to each to grasp their nearest hand and placed them on the object lying in her lap.

They both saw it at the same time, the minute they touched it.

"In my dream I had to rub my ring on it to see Aarvid," she said, indicating the book with her eyes and lifting her right hand to show off the coppery glow of the ring on her finger. "But, I was afraid to do it by myself because I also saw the scary man that way." She looked at both of them.

Before either one could interject a question, she briskly instructed, "Keep your hand on the edge of it and don't let go." Next, she placed her ring finger on the book's flat leather surface, making sure that the ring contacted its colorful cover, and started to rub it. Slowly, tenuously her hand moved back and forth."I hope its going to be Aarvid." she whispered, concentrating on the book.

"There! Watch closely."

Gemma could not believe her eyes. She had been surprised by the confidence Mona had shown in believing what she had seen in her dream to be true. However, something was indeed happening on top of the book's surface.

Detective VanderLinden had been greatly relieved at hearing that all the commotion was just about a dream. He knew how upsetting the whole experience had been and was humoring the youngster, watching her rub her little ring finger onto that large leather tome.

He could not believe his eyes when indeed something strange and unreal was happening on the surface that was being rubbed.

He observed at first a light mist that quickly turned darker. In it, two shapes were visible. They seemed to be inside some small confined space; actually, it looked somewhat akin to the interior of a tent, but it wasn't.

What dropped the detective's jaw in amazement were the voices. They could be heard so clearly, it was as if they were all inside that space together. When he looked at the intensely focused Mona, and next at her equally focused mother, he realized that they had recognized at least one of the voices.

A young boy's husky voice spoke, "…They think I am dangerous because I can do magic?"

Tears were coursing down Gemma's cheeks when she softly spoke through muted sobs, "My baby, my boy. He is alive!" She continued to listen avidly to the conversation that was taking place between the young boy and an adult woman.

What surprised the detective was the calm resignation in the voice of the youngster, who he now believed to be the missing Aarvid, while the two discussed the possibility of him being eliminated. From what he could gather watching the darkened scene, was that it was taking place in another dimension. Things just did not look the way you'd expect it. When the young voice spoke sadly, "…I miss my mom and my pesky little sister. I wish I was back at home…" both mother and daughter broke down.

When he uttered wistfully, "Maybe this is all just a bad dream and tomorrow when I wake up, everything will be back to the way it was," mother and daughter were barely able to hear the other's muted response: "You can't turn the clock back, Aarvid. We need to move on. I need you to be strong."

His resigned, almost defeated, "…OK…I'll try…" broke them down into uncontrolled hugs and sobs. As a result, Mona broke contact with the tome and the connection evaporated.

Suddenly, there were all sorts of questions that he would like an answer to. Instead, he listened to the exchange between mother and daughter.

Mona reiterated that what she had dreamed was real and that

Aarvid existed in some magic state that had reduced him to be small enough to fly on the back of a swan.

Gemma kept asking questions about Aarvid's companion and the two powerful beings that were pursuing them. Mona, who did not have the answers, just shrugged. Finally, mother and daughter had settled down enough to remember that the detective was there in the room with them and the questioning started anew.

Detective VanderLinden had silently concluded that what he had observed was real, too real to deny. Young Aarvid was indeed alive and had a companion willing to help him through tough times. He did not understand their relationship completely, other than that she appeared to be mentoring him and quite protective of him.

Mona's brother was in serious danger from two individuals who were pursuing both the young boy and his companion. He had never heard of this Cardinal Mephisto or something, and this other character Black Maggie David but he would search his files to see if something might turn up.

One thing he had a real problem with, but was willing to concede since it made everything that had happened easier to explain, Aarvid existed in another realm which made him invisible.

Finally, Mona had a conduit to her brother. Through her they could keep track of the boy.

He shared with them his conclusions which seemed to be especially hard on Gemma. When both mother and daughter appeared lost in their own quiet thoughts, he reflected on what he should do next with the information he had just gained.

What should be my next step in trying to retrieve the boy? Had a crime been committed? Was the boy in imminent danger?

He had no firm answers to those questions. What he did know was that he had made a promise to mother, daughter and to himself that he would do whatever it would take to bring Aarvid back to his family.

He decided he needed to sleep on it. So the detective got up from the edge of the bed and suggested they all get a bit more rest.

Mona grabbed his hand and moaned, "Don't go. What if that awful man comes back?"

Gemma, who was still wiping away the tears that had coursed down her cheeks added, "Why not stay here and sleep on the sofa, Detective?"

When he hesitated, she continued, "I would be more comfortable having you stay here tonight, if you do not mind."

He nodded in quiet acquiescence and then followed it with, "Maybe you are right. It would be better for all of us. Thanks."

CHAPTER 10
THE SOUND
OF THE GONG

BLAWAMM!! It was so loud and sounded so close by, Aarvid just about jumped out of his skin. With his heart pounding in his chest, and his mind instantly alert, he focused on the mind of any human in the area of the marsh. It did not even occur to him that he had reflexively used his telepathic abilities to identify the shooter. Awakened out of a sound sleep, he had jumped at the most immediate way to clear up his confusion.

"There are a flock of them out there!" Jenn exclaimed from the far side of their shelter. "I count at least six or seven of them." She sounded worried and upset.

"There are just a couple of them that want to shoot migrating waterfowl. One of them is looking especially for large geese or She did not have to ask how he knew. Yet, she was nevertheless impressed.

167

"Gons!" Aarvid exclaimed. "He is in danger! We've got to warn him!"

"You are doing pretty well so far, Aarvid." Her voice sounded like she had calmed down and it held a challenge. "Why don't you do that."

It did not take long before Aarvid let out a sigh of relief while stating, "I've located him. He is near a small island a long way out, away from this shore. There appear to be no hunters out there. I told him to stay put until we contact him. He seemed to be quite happy about that. It seems that he met another swan, a female. He said she had touched beaks with him."

Jenn was sitting on the edge of her bedding and was relieved to hear that the swan was safe. Something else had made her curious, however. Listening to him and seeing his outline in the filtered grey light of a wet and early dawn, he seemed different. He had taken charge immediately and he had not hesitated correcting her assessment.

She got up and walked over to where he sat on his bedding hugging his long, awkwardly crossed legs, with his chin resting on his knee. In the dim light he seemed bigger. His face, a slight smile playing across it, lifted up from its resting place on his knee to face her.

Jenn was looking at the face of a young man. It was very much Aarvid's face, yet it was much more mature.

The smile was quickly replaced by a more serious expression as he said, "He was not exactly thinking of coming over here. That lonely female seems to have captured his attention. He did not even seem to be interested in my news, just in whether she was equally interested in him." He paused for a moment, and then continued pensively, "I hope he'll come for us later."

With her eyes Jenn tried to asses how much he had changed

overnight, with her mind she was furiously thinking ahead. What could be their pursuers' next move? To Aarvid she said, "Aarvid, we need to think of leaving here. I am certain that your mental reaching out has alerted them to our location. Even your slightest use of the magic makes the magic virtually purr and vibrate. If I could feel that, then certainly one of the mages or one of their more sensitive lieutenants could, too."

Getting up from his bedding, his determined answer caught her somewhat by surprise. "We'll just have to fight them off again, Jenn. I would not ask Gons to risk getting himself shot. Besides, the fog will slow them down." He lifted one of the feathers and looked out underneath it before reiterating, "It's like pea soup out there. Near as I can tell, it looks like it is misting as well. Everything is absolutely drenched out there." Lifting the feather a little higher so she could peek out as well, he continued, "I think it would be better if we did not let ourselves get spooked into greater trouble."

For a moment, Jenn was lost for words. *My goodness,* she thought, *he has not noticed what has happened to him, but in that light he looks absolutely fantastic. Those muscles! He is now as tall as I am.*

She could not take her eyes off him but covered it by acting as if she was thinking. It helped, because she actually did find herself thinking about their situation. The distraction caused by the dramatic change in his appearance, coupled with the assurance in his response, had almost made her believe that things were quite in control. Her long experience told her not to let down her guard.

"Aarvid, as soon as we are able to, we should hunt up something to eat. Something tells me that this is going to be a very exciting day. I am certain that we can expect our friends to arrive shortly."

"Here, we have these." Aarvid had pulled out his stash of nuts and started to hand them to her, when she cut him short.

"No, no thanks, Aarvid. You'd better hang onto those and save them for emergencies. Besides, it may be necessary for us to eat on the fly later on, if we manage to get out of here that is."

She had no sooner uttered those words when, *BLAMM*...followed by a more distant *blawamm*, shattered the silence outside once again.

It was the second more distant discharge that had Aarvid worried. He probed mentally in both directions before concluding, "They have small boats. That one," he pointed at the source of the more distant blast, "I think he is heading toward Gons and his new friend."

After a moment's pause, he added, "We can't risk having something happen to them. I have no choice, I have to do something!"

"You are right. We might be able to hold of our pursuers for a time but eventually we'll have to find a way to escape. The big bird is our greatest ally." After a few moments of silence, she added, "How are you going to be able to help?"

Aarvid's expression was determined. With both hands pressing his temples he stalked around the small space. When he finally looked up, there was mischief in his eyes. "I have always been leery of dense fog. In my imagination I could always see images of strange things in it. I think I'll make it more real this time."

"What are you planning to do, Aarvid? You're not going to hurt anyone are you?"

"No," he answered snickering lightly, "I'll just scare them a little."

Aarvid quickly donned his warm vest, wrapped his cloth around his waist and strapped his sword to his back before lifting the feathers that covered their shelter. Outlined against the grey light of the foggy morning, Jenn could hardly believe how much her protégé had changed. The smooth, lean lines of the youth of yesterday were replaced by the solid muscled form of a young man. When she followed him out, she watched a determined young man standing at the edge of the nest under the shelter of a just barely visible leaf. His eyes scanned the fog that quickly settled on his hair and face. All around the two of them the dew droplets floated silently with the air currents, interrupted by an occasional splashing sound of large droplets falling from invisible leaves of marsh grass stretching above them.

Jenn leaned back against the firm quill of a feather that was part of their shelter's roof and tuned in on what Aarvid was doing.

"Gons!" In his worried state, the telepathic message was nearly deafening.

Before she had a chance to let him know he was overdoing it, the swan answered, "Hey, go easy!" It was followed by several images that she interpreted as, "You're causing me to ruffle my feathers. I don't want my new friend to think I am upset with her." The swan's final telepathic image was that of a delicately shaped, slightly smaller swan.

Aarvid continued in a slightly less overpowering way to convey what he was planning to do to make things save for the large bird and his companion. He added the urgent message that they themselves might be in need of being rescued before too long and asked the swan, "Please be there, when we need you."

While she was listening in on his mental conversation, Jenn took a good look at young Aarvid. He did resemble the eleven-year-old of yesterday in many ways. However, those similarities were superficial at best. In the soft light of this fog shrouded dawn she could clearly see the physical changes that she had missed earlier in the diffuse light of their shelter. Gone was the softness around the eyes and lips. Instead, there was strength and intelligence radiating from his fine features and large brown eyes. She found herself looking at a well build teenager with beguiling looks, who appeared to act with a confidence well beyond even the age of his looks. He seemed to have a clear grasp of the advantages and disadvantages of his plan as he explained it to the swan, using appropriate images in the process for the large bird's benefit.

As she listened to his plan unfold itself, she felt nearly overcome with relief and happiness. She had been beset with doubts whether she had done the right thing by committing young Aarvid to this dangerous path, even more so since she had come to know him as an endearing and caring eleven-year-old. Now, however, she knew that she had done the right thing, and that the changes that had taken place and those yet to come would bear out her faith in him.

When he was done instructing the large bird and turned to address her, she quickly moved closer to him, gently placed her hands on each side of his face, and looked directly into his eyes. "That is a wonderful plan, Aarvid." His soft brown eyes told her that he was pleased by her approval. As she let go of him, she continued, "The idea of turning the tables on the hunter and making sure that others who might harm the birds are herded to shore is very clever. I am very proud of how you got it all to come together."

As she turned away from him, she added, "While you carry out your plan, I'll go take a look to see what food I can gather us for breakfast. I should not be too long. Please wait here for me." She had moved a few steps toward the edge of the nest when she turned once more to add, "I just hope that they will be able to make it down here in time for us." With that, she jumped onto a broad green leaf and was gone into the myriads of floating fog droplets.

Manfred, who believed he was a pretty good hunter, was getting quite upset. The weather was cold and the fog was as dense a he had ever seen it here in the great marshes leading into the North Sea and near border with Dutch Friesland.

He had promised Frau Biederman a goose for dinner and twice now, he had missed his quarry completely. That blasted fog. The birds were out of the water and winging away before he could take proper aim. He was just hoping that his partner was having better luck. He was so done with sauerkraut and sausages.

Maybe if he poled his way over to that island over there, the fog would be less dense and he would be able to get off a better shot. Newly determined, he set his boots in his flat bottomed boat and pushed with his long pole.

He had not gone more than a few yards, when he entered a clearing in the fog bank. On the other side it seemed thicker than three day old pea soup, while in front of him a thin layer of swirling haze covered the slowly undulating water. He had just planted his pole into the sticky bottom when he saw something of gigantic proportions move in the fog bank ahead of him. Confused, he lifted his pole and let the boat drift while he watched. *Could it be a big boat?*

A light breeze touched his moisture soaked face. Suspicious of the movement and change in the air, Manfred wiped the wetness from his brow and face, blew away the droplets collecting on his considerable nose, and stared closely at the swirling motions in the approaching fog bank. The next moment, his jaw dropped from amazement. It was soon followed by a cramping in his stomach from the fear that suddenly overtook him. A giant, white, and curving neck had lifted out of the thick fog. It was attached to a huge goose head with hollow black eyes and a powerful beak that opened up as it rose out of the dense fog, revealing a sinuously moving tongue. On either side of the head two incredibly huge, white feathered wings rose up and fanned the thickly swirling fog under them. The monstrous goose-like apparition turned directly toward him and immediately headed his way. The way the thick layer of dense fog was stirring around above the water underneath those wildly flapping wings, its body must have been enormous.

Manfred, who was very superstitious, was convinced that he had upset some powerful dark force. It had taken the shape of the creatures he had been hunting to give them their revenge on him. It was now their turn to hunt him.

With a powerful expletive, he hurried to the other side of his skiff and pushed off at the same time. In his hurry, he had not properly set himself. Unbalanced, the small boat lurched and Manfred fell into the cold murky water, losing his favorite gun in the process.

In minutes he was back on the skiff, feverishly retrieved his pole, and frantically poled to get away from the monstrous goose pursuing him.

He could not move fast enough. Slowly the dense fog layer that hid the house-sized body of the towering creature advanced on him. As it approached, the hideous head lowered itself, preparing to gobble up the soaked and thoroughly chilled Manfred, so he thought.

When the fog enveloped him, Manfred poled on furiously,

absolutely convinced he had reached the last hour of his life. He thought he could hear the swirl of the wake created by the creature that pursued him, as well as an occasional moaning sound. Unfortunately, his teeth chattered so loudly, he could not be sure of what he was hearing. He was so cold he thought he would never be warm again. To add insult to injury, he had no idea if he was heading toward shore or toward open water.

When, surrounded by the white haze of fog, Manfred's skiff finally reached the shallows of what looked like a dark muddy beach, he abandoned his boat heedless of the treacherous mud and ran for all he was worth until his feet felt solid ground.

Out of the dense fog three other running shapes appeared. When they saw each other, they all slowed their run to a brisk walk and approached each other. Manfred recognized his friend and partner almost immediately, except that his face was deathly pale and he too was soaked and chilled to the bone.

Manfred pointed at the wet clothes and asked, "Accident?" His friend nodded. One of the others pointed at Manfred and repeated the question, "Accident?" They all laughed heartily trying to shake off the fear that had just moments ago gripped them all.

Aarvid sat back under the protection of a large green leaf. He felt pretty proud of himself. No one had been hurt and the hunters, along with some others who might have been crabbing or digging for clams, were safely herded away from this part of the marsh.

He suddenly realized that with all the excitement after waking from a sound sleep, he had not had the opportunity to relieve himself.

Standing on the edge of the slowly swaying nest, he fumbled around and…"My…What?" He left what he was going to say unfinished. There were no words for the shock and confusion that rocked him. He stood there for a few moments forgetting the purpose for his balancing act on the edge of the nest. He stepped back and inspected what just a moment ago he had thought could not possibly be his. But it was, as were the powerfully muscled legs that were holding him up.

Consternation, bordering on panic gripped his confused mind. Aarvid suddenly recalled Jen's statement from the day before, explaining why the denizens of the realm looked surreal and gruesome. She had said, "In this realm, people become who they really are. They cannot hide their true identities." He wondered, *Am I becoming some kind of freak?*

Careful to take in all details, Aarvid started to do a self inspection. He started with his hands, then his arms, next he felt and looked at what he could observe of his chest and stomach. He was amazed; none of it looked or felt like it had just the day before. From what he could gather, he must have grown into a well muscled young man.

During his self examination his panic slowly changed into curiosity, and then into excitement. He was now truly anxious to get a look at what he could not see, he needed a mirror. He remembered the puddle of water on the other side of the nest and quickly made his way there.

The reflection looking back at him was amazing and shocking at the same time. *Wow, that is me? I look like one of those big teenagers with all that muscle, and my face…If Anke could see me now.* He stood there transfixed, looking at himself, daydreaming about what Anke's reaction to his new self would have been.

Finally, Aarvid gathered himself and his thoughts went to Jenn. *I wonder if she noticed? …She must have.*

Suddenly, he realized that it had been a while and she had

not returned. Instantly alert to danger, he reached out to her with his mind.

Nothing! It was as if she had disappeared from the face of the earth. He repeated his effort with greater intensity and…There! He had made some kind of contact with her, but it was as if she was almost out of his reach. He probed for her location. She was not that far away. Aarvid realized something was very wrong. Jenn must be in serious trouble.

A wave of panic and self guilt swept over him. How long had she been in trouble while he had indulged in self exploration and fantasies? In a flash, he was off. Still busy strapping his sword to his back; he leapt off the edge of the nest, onto a broad sheath of green leaf. Navigating his way around the myriad of crystal clear droplets of water, he ran along its length. Next, like a mad man possessed, he leapt onto the ridges of a firm, yet swaying stalk and climbed up toward where he knew she must be.

Mona woke up with a start. What a weird dream she had had last night. She tried to remember, and in doing so realized that what she remembered had not been a dream at all. She had found a way to contact Aarvid, her brother.

When she tried to rub the sleep from her eyes, she noticed the ring on her ring finger. In the grey, early morning light that filtered through the screened window the copper ring glowed with a ruddy red color. The ring, along with the beautiful book, had given her the ability to make contact with her brother. She could clearly remember the scene it had shown her and how she had listened to him converse with that stranger. With the memories returning, fear did as well.

Mona remembered how the flame throwing creature had wanted possession of the magic book. *The magic book! Where is the book?* her mind screamed at her. Still groggy with sleep, she could not remember. She reached for it on her night stand next to her bed, but it was not there. Panicked, she sat up, wide awake.

She was about to yell for her mom, when she remembered. She had placed the book under the bed last night in an effort to hide it from anyone coming into her room while she slept.

Still fearful that it might not be there, Mona quickly retrieved the magic book from under her bed. Relieved to have it in her hands once again, she sat, hugging it, on the edge of her bed and studied her copper ring. She was amazed at how clearly she could make out the details of the figure engraved on it. Outlined in bright copper tones against a darker background, was the image of a multiple armed warrior. Mona was convinced it was the image of a prince out of a story she had yet to hear.

Anxious to know how her brother was doing, yet hesitant because she did not want to come face to face with "The Creature" again, she was just about to rub her ring onto the shiny bright leather surface, when her mom walked in carrying a steaming cup of hot chocolate.

"Honey, what is the matter? Why are you sitting there on the edge of your bed?"

Not waiting for an answer, she continued, "Here, have some hot chocolate. It'll pick you up." She handed Mona the steaming cup and sat down next to her.

Mona was getting used to the fact that others, including her mother, could not see the book unless they actually touched it. She was a little confused about why they kept forgetting about it, but she did not dwell on it. She enjoyed the feel of the warm liquid as it slid down her throat. It did make her feel more awake and it calmed the nervous fluttering of her stomach. After finishing the mug, she placed it on her bedside stand. With a, "Thanks, Mom," she hugged her mom, added a light kiss, and reached for her mother's hand. Mona placed her mother's hand gently on the corner of the leather tome. "I was just about to see about Aarvid. Remember, Mom? Remember how we saw him last night?"

Instantly aware of the book Gemma was eager to see her son again. Yet, when Mona started to bring her ringed hand down to the book, she felt fear rising in her throat. "Wait! Wait for just another minute, dear!"

Gemma was not quite sure she wanted to know. She felt anxious anticipation. *What if something had gone wrong?* She realized instantly that she would want to know.

After a deep breath she said, "OK, go ahead, dear. Let us see how he is doing." She huddled close to her daughter, all the while holding the corner of the tome. "You're sure it is going to work?"

Large broad and flat green swaths ran back and forth across the vision. On one of those a young man moved rapidly, jumped to a rough stalk and ran across another. The young man was well muscled and moved with the agility and grace of a well trained athlete. He leapt from one green swath onto another, until he reached what looked like a netted cache of cylinder shaped cocoons.

Not comprehending what it was they were watching, yet aware of the urgency in the young man's movements, Mona and her mom watched breathlessly. They watched in puzzlement as the young man inspected the large cocoons through the netting. Having decided on one, he pulled a long blade from its cover on his back and sliced through the netting. Next, with the long blade emitting barely visible blue sparks, he carefully sliced open one of the cocoons. To their consternation, it contained a young woman. After the young man peeled away the pale white sheathing of the cocoon, the woman lay limp and pale on the green surface next to the pile of remaining cocoons.

"I don't know…What are we looking at?" stammered Mona, confused because she had fully expected to see her brother in the scene unfolding on top of the book in her lap. Something else had added to her confusion; initially, before they could clearly see the young man, she had felt certain it had been her brother. It had just felt like him and even now, looking at the strange young man, it still did.

"I do not know who that is," answered Gemma. "It sure looks like those are giant blades of…eh…could it be some sort of grass?" She answered her own question. "Yes, they are! And either those plants are giant sized, or the people in them are so small, they must be nearly invisible."

After a short pause, Gemma pointed at a corner of the screen. Alarmed, she said, "There! You see that dark thing hiding under that large leaf? From the number of legs and the way it moves, it looks like a giant spider." Next, she pointed at the young man and the prone form of the young woman and added, "Mona, you know what I think?" When Mona looked at her askance, she continued, "I think that that young man just saved that woman's life. If I did not know any better, I'd say that that spider—it looks almost the size of a small bus—must have had her trapped, and meant to have that woman for dinner. Those cocoons over there are other prey it has captured."

"Mom, Mom, look at that spider now! It is coming out from under that leaf!" When her mother let out a small gasp instead of answering, Mona gave her a quick glance. Her mother's mouth had dropped open in surprise and she was staring fixated at the scene. But not where the spider was stealthily approaching; she was looking at the young man. He was now looking straight back at them.

When Mona finally refocused on the strapping young man, she felt totally thrown off balance. That face and the way he smiled. It was almost as if he could see them. Mona knew it then, it had felt like Aarvid before; now that they had a connection, there was no doubt. "It IS Aarvid!" she gasped.

Almost at that same instant, Gemma, who had recognized him as well, moaned, "My son. What happened to you, baby?"

Mona could hear him say it while Gemma could read it from his lips. "I love you," he said slowly, looking straight up at them and smiling. "I love you, Mona, and I love you, Mom," he repeated slowly, almost miming the words.

"He knows we're here!" Gemma stated it, because it was all so unbelievable she needed to hear herself say it. "What happened to him? He looks like he is sixteen and so big and muscular. Who is that woman…?"

"Mom…Aarvid, look out! Behind you! The spider!" Mona yelled out. She could see Aarvid flinch and duck with her warning.

In a flash, the large body flew through the air, knocking Aarvid off his feet in the process, and landed some distance past the prone pair. Aarvid struggled to get back on his feet, but something kept him from getting up.

Sick with worry, Mona leaned forward. As she did, the picture zoomed in on her prone brother. There it was! A thick, clear, sticky and ropelike substance kept him nailed to the green surface. She realized it was something the spider had done to him.

Mona and her mother watched helplessly while Aarvid struggled to reach his sword. It was just beyond his reach.

Slowly, deliberately the spider turned and moved toward his new prey.

Aarvid was beside himself with worry. Fortunately, in spite of her weak response to his urgings, he did not experience any problems locating Jenn. In his hurry, he nearly blundered past the stack of netted cocoons. When it became clear to him that she was trapped inside one of them, he quickly probed each of them to establish which one of the many cocoons she occupied. Aarvid felt energized with hope when his magically enhanced sense pinpointed her; her mind was responding weakly, but it was responding. She was still alive.

After Aarvid freed her from the entrapment of the cocoon, he felt renewed worry at the way she looked; she was deathly pale and her skin felt so cold to his touch. What gave him hope was to see her breasts rise and fall in a slow, but rhythmic breathing. While he was busying himself with his partner, something else intruded on his awareness. He forced it aside until he was certain that his partner was not getting any worse. Only then did he allow himself to be distracted.

Aarvid realized immediately what had been tugging on his awareness. He knew that his sister and his mother were there somewhere looking in on him. He did not know how, but his mind recognized their confusion. He was doubly pleased, when he felt the change in their emotions when they realized it was him. *They know me! Even now they know me!*

Almost immediately after Aarvid uttered the words, "…I love you, Mom," he felt a sudden spike in fear accompanied by a shouted warning coming from Mona. Her warning temporarily saved him from the spider's deadly embrace. His quick response allowed him to avoid full contact with the bulky form of the spider as it hurtled itself at him. The small, poison injecting mouth parts with their debilitating venom barely missed him. Unfortunately for Aarvid, the massive body of the jumping spider made enough contact to knock him down, while an ejection of the sticky rope-like substance from its posterior gland held him firmly rooted to the surface. No matter how hard he strained against the flexible green surface below him, he could not budge. He could just barely raise his head, just enough to see that his sword lay just a few feet away. If he could just reach it with his free hand, he could then cut himself free. If not, at least he would be able to defend himself. Unfortunately, no matter how hard he struggled, he could not reach it.

Helpless, Aarvid watched as the spider turned slowly and deliberately, to come face to face with him. Filled with dread, he saw it raise its triple eyed head with two fang-like hairy mouth parts that contained the dreaded poison. He must avoid those at all cost, or he and Jenn would both end up spider food. Worst of all, his sister and his mother were watching. Even though every muscle in his new body was burning from the strain, Aarvid gave it one more all out try. It felt as if he was tearing away the flesh from his back, but he kept on. He could feel his arm move. He could see it almost touching the sword.

The spider, sensing that his prey was trying to get away, took a small jump toward him. Aarvid knew it was preparing for a final attack. Gathering his focus, he willed his sword to come to him, to magically slide into his outstretched hand.

At that very instant, he heard Mona. It was as if she was right beside him shouting, "No!! You get away from him!"

Mona lifted her ring-hand off the tome. That spider would have to deal with her before it could do harm to her brother. Shouting, "Get away from him!" she punched down on it's image with her ring. For a brief moment, the ring sparkled blue. Next, the scene on top of the tome turned foggy and disappeared slowly.

"What is happening? What is happening to my son?" Gemma sobbed. She hugged her small daughter, who started to cry as well.

"Maybe I killed it," Mona said softly, not at all sure of herself. "I wanted to kill it. Maybe I did."

"You think so?" Gemma asked through sobs. "You really think so?" She wanted to believe. But, how could that possibly be? Only because of the book had they been able to see Aarvid. They were not really there. "Oh, Aarvid," with doubts assailing her, tears came anew. "My beautiful son, and so grown up. Please, please let him be all right," she pleaded through a mouthful of sobs.

Mona pulled away from her mother. Something was bothering her and she tried to remember what it was. Just before the scene had clouded over, she had felt something happening over where her brother was engaged in his struggle. It had to do with her ring. It had all happened too quickly for her to register what she had felt and seen with certainty. Mona focused inwardly trying to remember. *There was that funny feeling in my head. It was as if I was there.*

For a brief moment Mona had felt a powerful surge of mental awareness. She had felt connected to her brother in a very powerful way; she had felt his despair almost like it had been her own. It was followed almost immediately by a glimpse of some dark skinned being. It was an image of something or someone she had seen before but she could not place it. She mused, *It had looked like a...a...warrior? Yes! That's it! It's the warrior, the same one that's on my ring!* She was not certain, but it had felt to her as if the warrior had taken some of her emotion with him. The more she thought about it, the more certain she felt that the warrior and she were connected; he was there because of her.

"Mom, I think something happened because of my ring."

"I know, honey, I want him to be safe also." Gemma wiped the drying tears from Mona's face and continued, "But Aarvid is not really there. Maybe we just want to see him very badly, but what we see is not real and is not really happening." She took a deep breath. "Maybe Aarvid is perfectly safe…"

"Mom! I felt it! Something happened!" Resolutely she repositioned the tome in her lap from where it had slipped between her and her mother. "Let's look and see. Something happened. I am sure of it," she repeated, becoming more certain every time she said it. Just before Mona could bring her ringed hand down onto the book, Gemma grabbed her hand. With her own hand now touching the tome, Gemma instantly remembered what had seemed like a confusing nightmare just moments before. Now, as her hand touched the book, she remembered in detail the source of her dread.

Her face still wet with tears, she looked pleadingly at her daughter. "Please, wait! Not yet! What if something has happened to him?" She wiped at the wet stains with her free hand. "I don't know if I can stand to see it."

"Mom! What if he needs us?" Mona sounded more determined than ever. "What if something is happening and he needs my help?"

"How can you help him?" Emphasizing the "you," Gemma sounded as if she was ready to break down.

Mona looked her mother straight in the eye, raised her ringed finger and said, "I felt it, Mom. This ring, I felt it do something."

Gemma sighed resigned, placed her head on her daughter's

shoulder and whispered, "Go ahead and try, honey. At least we'll know."

An arc of blue lightning descended right to where his sword was lying. With it came a powerful mental surge, he recognized as his sister's. It was followed by a blinding flash. When Aarvid's eyes could see again, he was looking at the back of a bronze-brown skinned warrior, roughly twice his own size, wearing only a very short, elaborately embroidered loincloth. The warrior's six arms, flashed swords identical to Aarvid's. They twirled and slashed in rapid succession at the bulky form of the spider. When finally, the bronze skinned warrior turned toward Aarvid, the spider's oozing parts were scattered all around.

The tall well proportioned man smiled benignly at Aarvid. With kind eyes and a slight smile on his near perfect face, he nodded slowly at him and pointed one of his six armed arms at him. Aarvid understood and remained motionless. His eyes could just barely discern the quick slashing motion of the arms. However, the quick, feathery release of his binds that accompanied the rapid swooshing sounds, indicated to him that the six armed warrior had slashed through the thick, cord-like spider webbing that had held him captive, with surgeon-like precision,

Sore from his futile struggles to regain freedom, Aarvid struggled to his feet and reached out to shake hands with one of the many arms. Halfway through the motion, he stopped and looked up to the sky. He knew what was coming next. The sound could be heard more clearly every second; it was the sound made by a swarm of yellowjackets. He had been found. Their pursuers had caught up with him and his nearly unconscious partner.

At the sound of the approaching yellowjackets, the multi-armed warrior turned and looked skyward also. When the yellow and black banded insects continued to draw near, he raised his six sword-wielding arms and prepared his own attack.

Aarvid was astounded at the smooth coordinated movements of the three pairs of swords wielded by his tall protector. He had just a moment to wonder, *Where on earth did he come from?* The next instant, he saw how six skillfully wielded swords quickly cut down three of the approaching yellowjackets that ventured a little too close.

The insect's body parts and their mounted riders tumbled to the soft ground far below. The remainder pulled up quickly and moved rapidly away. As he watched the carnage and the scattered flight of the rest of his pursuers, Aarvid realized that his sister and mother had been absent during the short skirmishes, because he could discern their presence once again.

Aarvid could clearly feel their concern. His sister's much stronger felt emotions were more of a mix between curiosity and concern. He looked up and smiled at them once again. He could clearly feel his sister's pride in what she felt she had accomplished. It was then that he realized where that fantastic multi-armed warrior had come from. It puzzled him how Mona had managed to accomplish that and intensify the mental connection between them as well. A warm sense of pride and renewed love for both of them welled up in him. When he had faltered, nearly forgetting about his own abilities to use the magic that was available to him, his sister had come through and provided his protector.

Bwong! The loud strangely muffled church bell startled him. It seemed like the sound had come right from inside his head. Still, he turned thinking it might have emanated from his bronze skinned savior. To his surprise, the warrior had disappeared. Where he had been only a moment earlier, his sword lay still sizzling small blue sparks that slowly died down.

Aarvid picked up his weapon, sheathed it and quickly moved over to where Jenn was lying.

Still deathly pale, she had propped herself up on one elbow. There was renewed life in the eyes that looked at him quizzically. With words slurred by a mouth still slack from the poison, she said, "Fyeou arre fful off sprrisses farn't fyeou?"

"Sshh," he shushed her, pressing his finger to his lips before gently helping her to sit up. "We'll talk when you are feeling better."

Gently lifting her onto his shoulder, he continued, "We've been found. For now I think they'll leave us alone, but we'd better be on our way."

With Jenn's slack form draped across his shoulder, Aarvid turned toward where he could feel his mother's and his sister's presence, smiled, once more speaking and miming the words, "I love you. I have to go." He took a step, hesitated and looked up once more, "Mona, I know it was you! Thanks! Keep in touch if you can."

Her response just about blew him away. It was as if it came from right next to him. "I will, Aarvid, my big brother," interrupted by a small sniffle, she spoke softly in a voice filled with love for him.

Much more distant, he could hear his mother's choked voice saying, "I love you, my son. Please be careful."

Aarvid gave a quick wave and was off and running. Next, while leaping from leaf to leaf, always going down toward the edge of the water where it splashed onto the muddy soil, he contacted Gons.

To his pleasant surprise, the swan and his new companion were already waiting for him.

David, the Black Mage was furious. "Crawitz, I told you not to let your men get too close. I did not want the youngster and his partner to get spooked."

Crawitz stumbled all over himself trying to apologize for the gaffe. "…I instructed them to get close without being seen. It must have been the fog hanging over that swamp. They failed to see the young man and his partner until they were almost on top of them. We did not expect to be attacked by that…eh…dark-skinned giant of a warrior with sword-wielding arms sprouting…"

"An avatar of a Hindu god, that is what that warrior is called," David interrupted his commander.

"What did you just call that monstrous, death dealing dervish?" Burgher Jan piped in. He had been standing off to the side, trying not to draw too much attention and hoping that in all the confusion of the nearly disastrous moment, they had not noticed that it had been his doing that had led the flight of the company too near to the scene where the dark skinned multi-armed warrior had been waiting for them. He had been so preoccupied with concern for Jenn, seeing her lay there, deathly pale and near helpless next to that other young man, that he had guided his yellowjacket too close. The others had simply followed his lead. Burgher Jan had just barely avoided being beheaded by the whir of blue flashing blades. He had been fortunate that his mount escaped unharmed as well, or he would now be trying to extricate himself from the soft, sticky muck down on the ground far below.

"It is a reincarnation of an Indian deity," David continued in a murmur as if he was more talking to himself than trying to address Burgher Jan's query. Totally absorbed in distant memories, he mumbled pensively, "Maybe it was Balaji, the warrior avatar. How in heaven's name did he pull that one off?"

"A Balaji? What is a Balaji?" Burgher Jan pressed, frustrated at not having a clue as to what David was mumbling about. "More important, how did it get here? And how did that youngster know about that kind of Indian deity?" Then, looking at Burgher Jan, David continued, "It is part of a far eastern religion. Buddhism I believe. The deities have the ability to take on a number of human forms; they are the avatars of that deity."

David seemed to have spent his anger and stared off into the fog in the direction of where they had just met that deadly warrior and that young man. He was faced with a puzzle. Everything about the magic that had been used had indicated to him that that young man was the same one as that young boy, Aarvid. However, his eyes could not possibly have deceived him to that extent. That was no eleven-year-old he had seen standing next to that dark bronze warrior. And, to magically create that warrior avatar suggested magical abilities far beyond even his wildest imaginings. Although, he thought he had sensed another presence. *I just cannot be certain. There was a sudden shift in the magic. That magical jolt came so sudden, so unexpected.*

He paced around lost in thought, scratching his bearded face. *And then, that gong...What was that all about?*

Crawitz coughed softly to remind the Black Mage of his presence. At the sound, David turned to face him. "Commander, it looks like events have dictated a change in plans. I have decided to proceed alone with Burgher Jan. You are to collect your men and return with them to your home base. I will try to keep in touch." David paused, and then continued, "I want you to give this message to the Cardinal." He waited until Crawitz nodded his readiness. Then speaking slowly and emphatically, he said, "Your Eminence, caution and patience are your best allies." The Black Mage repeated his message to the commander, and waited for Crawitz to repeat it to himself and come to attention. While the commander remained at attention, David turned and walked to a yellow jacket waiting a few paces away. Burgher Jan followed his lead and headed for his insect mount. A few moments later they were off and disappeared into the thinning fog.

Detective VanderLinden had traveled north, north-east on a hunch. After listening to Mona's description he thought he had a pretty good idea of the direction the swan was flying in. He was heading toward the northern border area between Dutch Friesland and the north-west corner of Germany.

The detective had left the house early this morning and gone straight to his office to catch up with any messages, and to leave one for his boss. He hoped it would not upset his superior officer too much, but he felt he had no choice. In addition to the fact that he was befuddled as well as fascinated by this case, he had made a promise to that very attractive mother and her endearing daughter. Besides he had not taken any vacation in nearly a year. Rob felt he was due some time off. His note read:

Sir,
Please forgive me for my sudden departure. I have reasons to believe that I have a good lead on a kidnapping that occurred just last night.
I might be gone for an unspecified number of days. I may be out of touch for long periods of time. Please take it out of my vacation time if that is your pleasure. I'll update you when I have more facts to provide. The report with the specifics on this case is attached to this note.

Sincerely,
Rob VanderLinden...etc.

It was now nearing the middle of the day. The detective found himself driving into a small German coastal town, just about 15 minutes from the Dutch border. The sign, "Gilded Hand," showing a gold painted hand holding a frothing stein, swung lazily in the soft breeze. It reminded him that he had a terrible thirst and that his stomach was growling from hunger as well.

He pulled his car into the small parking lot, parked it, and got out. Rob VanderLinden was surprised to find the small pub already partially filled with patrons. It was pleasantly warm inside and the bartender who greeted him with a warm welcome and pleasant smile immediately asked what he would have to drink while he handed him a small lunch menu. Rob seated himself on the spacious bar next to a threesome of customers involved in an animated discussion. While he studied the lunch menu, he could not keep from overhearing the nature of the discussion.

"…It was after me. Larger than a good size barn, it was about to swallow me up, I'll tell ye…"

At first he thought it to be rather funny, three grown men arguing about whether a swan could not only be visible from three totally different areas within the spacious bay, in the middle of a dense fog, but also chase and threaten each of them. His interest was really peaked when he realized that the three were seriously comparing notes on the nature of the swan. Apparently it was a beast of enormous proportions, large and sufficiently threatening to have scared all three, along with a couple of others, right out of the marshes. When, two of the three taking part of the discussion admitted that they had actually been hunting for large water fowl, something clicked inside of his head.

Of course, it has to be something or someone using magic. How else to explain this scenario happening simultaneously at different locations in a large marsh? And that youngster, had he not flown off on the back of a swan? He found himself interested enough to ask the threesome some questions. When they discovered that he was not laughing at their misadventure, the detective found himself deluged with detailed stories from all three of them. In the end they only confirmed his suspicion, which he kept to himself, that magic had indeed been used to scare off the hunters. That meant that very likely the young man he was chasing had indeed been in this area.

While he ate his tasty lunch of sauerkraut and sausages topped off with a foaming tankard of beer, he probed the hunters with questions about the migrating habits of geese and swans. The hunters, who had warmed up to him after his interest in their stories, proved quite knowledgeable and provided him several scenarios for routes of migration of swans.

Pleasantly filled with food and feeling better informed, the detective set off and headed eastward, toward the most likely route of southern migration for swans and geese. While he fell in with the traffic, he reflected, *At any case, this will be a pleasant change of pace from the daily humdrum of shuffling paperwork.*

After traveling a few miles, he reminded himself, *Oh, yes. This is probably a good time to check in with the widow and her daughter. They will be pleased to hear the good news.*

Next, he dialed their number on his cell phone.

Far south, near where the southernmost coast of Ukraine met the Black Sea, on a hill overlooking a gently sloping valley, the spirit of the guardian of the magic, Ba El Shebub was rudely

193

awakened. The sound of the gong had reverberated along the lines of magic that connected his spirit to its source. It was that sound that raised it from its slumber inside the bole of the old tree on the hill top.

What? Already it has happened? Carefully, Ba El Shebub checked the events that had brought about the sounding of the Gong; to Ba's magic it indicated a momentous event. After reflecting on what the magic made clear to him, he was puzzled. *Could it be? They have melded? It cannot be true. They are both too young and have just barely come into the magic. Then again, why else would the gong strike if not for the passing of such a magnanimous event?* Ba's spirit paused its musing and once again tested the magic. *Yes indeed,* his spirit concluded. *It has happened. Let us reflect for a moment on the passage...It was so long ago...Yes that was it.*

Falling back on a memory that went back nearly 5000 years, Ba's spirit recited:

When there shall be more than one chosen by the magic to do the wielding, they shall meet and one shall conquer and prevail, or both shall smite one and the other. Should the chosen ones fail to challenge one another, they must commit to the melding. Thus, they shall be equally gifted with the power, or they may choose their roles according to their melding. This be the first of the requirements before the magic be fully committed.

Still, the spirit of Ba felt troubled. *Woe to those who dare to oppose them. I fear in the spirit of their youthfulness they may not be prepared to have such power.* After a moment's pause, his spirit shrugged mentally. *Alas, it is done.*

Resigned, it put aside its reservations. *The first of the requirements has been satisfied. The magic has chosen well up to this time. Let us hope that the chosen innocents will be well guided. So far, it appears that the boy and his sister will be doing well together.* The spirit sighed relieved. Pleased with itself, Ba El Shebub's spirit resumed its slumber.

The next morning, before resuming his voyage east, Rob VanderLinden picked up a local newspaper, *DAS VOLKSTAG.* After a cursory scan of the headlines, his eye fell on a short article on page 2; the headline really peaked his interest. He sat down and read:

Giant Swan haunts North-shore fishermen and clam diggers.

A strange event happened yesterday morning during the early morning hours to a number of fishermen and clam diggers, and we believe also to some of the local water fowl hunters. According to eyewitnesses, a giant-sized swan, some say it was the size of a large house, making hissing and threatening noises, cleared most of the wetlands and fishing-accessible coastal waters of its two-legged invaders.

As our witness Manfred Bittner described it to us, "It was coming out of this thick fog bank making hissing sounds and coming right at me. I dropped all my fishing gear and jumped off my boat into the water. It was as big as a house. If I had not lost my boots in the mud, I would have run through the swamp until I hit the shore. As it was, I had to climb back onto my skiff and the giant creature was almost on top of me. The eyes were coal black and real scary and the head kept bobbing up and down with its beak wide open. I was lucky to get out of there alive."

We did note that our man Manfred did not carry any fishing equipment. His attire was more like that of the local hunters who hunt for waterfowl. Could this be the revenge of the giant fowl for all the deeds done to its unsuspecting brethren?

What disturbed him about the article was that he suddenly was reminded of what could happen at home if the news reporters got a hold of his or Maarten's reports detailing Aarvid's disappearance. How would that poor, grief-stricken widow and her precocious little girl deal with the notoriety?

Volume one, The Sound of the Gong, ends here.

Next

Volume two, Madman's Poison

Printed in the United States
53619LVS00002B/115-126

9 781413 795776